IKE

To my good friends

Bob Godsey

IKE

A Firefly Life

By
Bob Godsey

PublishAmerica
Baltimore

First printing

At the specific preference of the author, PublishAmerica allowed this work to remain exactly as the author intended, verbatim, without editorial input.

This is a work of fiction set in a background of history. Public personages both living and dead may appear in the story under their right names. Scenes and dialogue involving them with fictitious characters are of course invented. Any other usage of real people's names is coincidental. Any resemblance of the imaginary characters to actual persons, living or dead, is entirely coincidental.

ISBN: 1-4241-3972-4
PUBLISHED BY PUBLISHAMERICA, LLLP
www.publishamerica.com
Baltimore

Printed in the United States of America

Ike looked at the stubs of his legs showing below his hospital gown. He was feeling tired today. Breathing was labored. It was like trying to breathe through a soda straw. It had been an effort to swing the stumps of his wasted legs over the edge of the bed even with the help of the, sometimes present, male nurse. *Goddamn! What a way to have to live. I hate this damn wheel chair. What a dumb thing to have to live with. I guess I had no choice. Doc just wouldn't risk general anesthesia. Lungs and heart are too weak. Damn! I can still hear that saw cutting through the bone. I thought, "Well, there it goes." ... And my toes itch and my ankles ache ... Why would I be feeling like that? ... Sure wish I could scratch my toes.*

The searing light of the July morning streamed invitingly into the bleak ward of Veteran's Hospital, Dayton, Ohio, reflecting off the daily-mopped tile floor reflecting gray on gray light onto the ceiling and the west wall. It would be a great day to be outside. How Ike longed to get out into the sun and feel the life-giving warmth again. The brief visits on the verandah in his wheel chair

5

were less frequent now. It had become more difficult to go out with each passing day. This last week had been particularly difficult. Here it was, the first week in July and he hadn't felt strong enough to do anything.

The racking phlegmatic cough started again, as it did each morning. It would last through most of the day. His stomach and back muscles ached from the spasms of endless coughing. Though fatigue was weakening every muscle of his body, the spasms came with surprising intensity. His back and stomach muscles screamed with pain.

Tired, tired, God almighty, I'm tired. I don't know if I have ever been this tired in my life… Well, I guess, when I think about it, I can remember many times when I wasn't sure I could go another step. That brings back lots of memories.

The small RCA tabletop radio was playing softly. The morning news was about the same as usual. Local Dayton news of auto wrecks, robberies, financial news, weather, and an up-date on the Cincinnati Reds.

The radio droned on: [Six 'death row' inmates tried to break out of San Quentin…two guards were taken hostage…tear gas was used to put down the escape try. The guards were released with only minor injuries.]…[Winston Churchill is recovering nicely from a broken hip suffered in a fall]. [Nikita Khrushchev warned the U.S., "Any attack of China by Chang Kaishek would receive full retaliation from the Communist block countries.]… [The U.S. Senate began debate on a national health bill for the aged today.]…[The Reds split a double header with the Chicago Cubs. Banks headed up the first game with a bases loaded grand slam homer. First game Cubs five Reds four, but the Reds came back winning four to three in the second. Reds now standing fifth in the league with a forty-one to thrity-five win loss record.]

Ike had probably seen only two pro baseball games in his life, but there in the Dayton Hospital, one had to be a Cincinnati fan. It was the frequent conversation of the day. The news faded into the background of his mind as Ike remembered an earlyMay day in Scott County, Virginia recalling the fatigue he had felt from their long move out of Appalachia he recalled.

* * * *

"Ike, get your ass in gear and help Ma get some things carried out to the wagon. We gotta get this wagon headed out as soon as we can."

"Sure Pa, I was just headed up thar to help a spell."

William Godsey's tall angular frame, spoke of a man who was beaten. The little slump of the shoulders under the blue cotton workshirt revealed this truth. His blue denim bibbed coveralls were patched in the knees. The pockets were frayed, and small patches of tobacco juice stain decorated the bib. His dark straight hair, high cheekbones, and substantial broad nose bespoke his Cherokee blood from his grandmother.

Brother Bob and William had put the left front wheel of the wagon on a makeshift block while they inspected the wheel rim. William said it had a right mind to get loose on the wheel.

Brothers Walt and Sylvester were in the barn feeding, currying, and harnessing the mules. Sister Maude was helping Ma gather personal belongings to pack on the wagon. Brother Joe was sacking corn for the mules, and had pulled out two bales of hay to be hung on the back of the wagon. In no way could they take enough food for the mules and still have the room they needed for the family's personal property. Most all the furniture had to be left behind and it had been given to neighbors who had much need any kind of household furnishings.

There was no way the family of six kids and two adults could survive the economic conditions as they were. They could not grow enough tobacco on their twenty-acre plot, which they rented from a local banker in Hilton. The corn crop barely produced enough food for the mules and two cows. The cows had to be sold to provide money for the big move.

One of William's friends had returned from the area near Richmond, Indiana, with a report of plentiful jobs available. Farmers were hiring hands to work the fields, and new factories were starting up and hiring. It had looked like a good idea, particularly since the friend gave William the name of a farmer to contact upon arrival.

William and Rhoda had discussed their situation during the winter and decided to leave before spring planting. It would take them about five weeks, with good luck, to reach their Promised Land. They could follow Wilderness Trail, as blazed out by Daniel Boone, across Cumberland Gap and northward through central Kentucky.

Ike ran to the house to get a box of canned meat Rhoda had put up during the winter. The house wasn't much. Some of the floorboards were broken and the roof shingles were curled and covered with algae. The porch roof pulled away from the house on the south end. The house was weatherbeaten, much in need of paint, and would need fixing up before another tenant could be asked to move in. But, it had been home for Ike over the past ten years. There was a lump in his throat as he stood there.

He looked about from the house. The front porch overlooked the fog-filled valley offering a pleasant view on clear days. Their too-small house was built on a slope overlooking the tree-lined creek, which emptied onto the broader valley below. Their valley was narrow, with sharply rising walls on the east and west sides. Red bud and dogwood were in bloom, and mountain laurel colored the hillsides. Seven miles to the south, their valley opened into Little Moccasin Creek and the Old Wilderness Road at Gate City. Many thousand settlers had used Wilderness Road as they streamed into Kentucky and the new country west of the mountains.

Ike wondered what the new country to the north would be like. He was sure the land was flatter, the fields bigger, but it couldn't be as pretty as this country.

The treasured cedar chest, with most of the family's clothing, had already been loaded. Smaller boxes had been filled with all the sundry needs of food, tools, and provisions necessary for the long journey ahead. All were quickly loaded.

As Joe dragged the two bales of hay to the wagon, Walt and Sylvester brought the harnessed mules, attached the singletrees, and attached the front of the tongue to the collars. The wagon was off the block now. It was time for all to get on board. No one was in a happy mood. Ike noticed a lone tear on Rhoda's face. William's lips were drawn tight in a look between determination and pain.

Bob, being the youngest, sat on the spring board seat between William and Rhoda. Maude rode on a pile of blankets near the front of the wagon. The rest of the boys sat on the tailgate for awhile. The road out of the holler was a rutted lane for some of the time, but the exit was down the middle of the dry creek bed. The bouncing was soon too much for the boys' skinny butts and they soon began walking behind.

The older boys were going to be like William who was tall, lanky, and dark-featured with the hint of the Cherokee lineage. Bob was too young at this time to know just what his stature would be. The boys had been raised in the rough and tumble world of the mountains, learning to make do with what they had, and being grateful when each new day dawned. The boys were rough and ready—early to smoke, and more than a few times they would hit the jug of good ol' mountain jack. Ike was too young to be drinking at this time, but he remembered sneaking to the jug several times to test the syrupy hot mixture.

Rhoda was a hardened, mountain woman. Her countenance was severe. She was a strict disciplinarian and never joked about anything. Her words were few, but she meant what she said, and she spoke truth. Her black hair was pulled back in a tight bun. Her angular body was usually clad in a cotton print dress. Though it did not show outwardly, she had a tenderness and commitment to family and home. Ike remembered seeing that tear on Ma's cheek as she walked down the lawn to get on the wagon. He never saw her look back.

Hilton Station was just down the road a piece, and they were soon there. Hilton had a nice new passenger station on a spur line of the Atlantic & Ohio Railroad. The spur ran north and south through the narrow valley. Several old friends greeted them as they drove through. William had taken care of all his business the day before in order to avoid being held up today. He wanted to get as far along the road as possible. They were tempted to stop and "chat a spell", but they needed to put miles behind them. The mules were fresh at this point and it would be easier going when they reached Old Wilderness Road, and William wanted to get as far as Clinchport if they could.

Little Moccasin Creek had provided a pathway for the Atlantic & Ohio Railroad and the Wilderness Road. They stopped at noon to water the mules. William let the team graze along the creek bank running beside the rutted road, allowing them enjoy some of the long roadside grass. By late afternoon they had reached Clinchport on the Clinch River.

Walt and Sylvester took care of the mules, as was their job. Pa helped Ma put up the tarps at the sides and back of the wagon. Maude got the food out. Joe worked on building a fire near the wagon. Ike and Bob went down at the river skipping flat stones in the water. That didn't last long though. William was quick to let them know they had to help with the daily routine.

In Clinchport, William met Mr. Scott, a freight hauler. He suggested we follow him a day or so. He would be staying in Middlesboro for a few days, and would welcome the company, since William felt they could benefit from Mr. Scott's knowledge of Wilderness Road. After crossing the Clinch at Speers Ferry, they traveled down Powell Valley about forty-five miles and then across Cumberland Gap. The road across the "Gap" was rugged, although it had been traveled by hundreds of thousands of settlers over the past hundred years or so. It was rutted, rocky, and difficult for wagon travel.

While going up the steep grades, everyone but the driver

would get out of the wagon to lighten the load for the mules. On occasion, the family would even push the wagon. Going down grade was just as bad, for the wagon tended to run up on the mules. The back wheels were braked with large crescent-shaped wooden blocks bolted to mounts operated by a large lever on which the driver place his foot pressing the brakes against the wheel rims. It was an exhausting ordeal when going down some of the long rutted trails. The softness of the roadway helped much of the time, but the driver had to exert great force to keep the load from running into the mules and spooking them.

The way through the mountains was on foot unless the roadway ran along a stream where it was fairly level and the mules could pull the load. Ike remembered the exhaustion he had felt. Each day brought the same feeling of not being able to go any further. Each day they planned to cover a least twenty miles. Most days they would be able to go further. Much of the trail ran near streams through valleys long used by the many Indian tribes hunting in this, their "ancient hunting grounds".

He remembered some bridges across minor creeks. Yellow Creek had to be forded several times during the second week as they headed north from Middleboro. Walt and Sylvester would have to lead the mules across holding tightly to the bridle. The mules hated stepping into the stream.

Their trail led them through Pineville, Barbourville, Corbin, London, Pine Hill, and into Berea, their stop-over place. The left front wheel rim finally needed the attention of a blacksmith. It would be good to let the mules get a couple days rest. The family made camp in the field near the blacksmith shop.

All the kids were surprised to find a college in the mountain

town of Berea. They had never heard about a college where all the
students were mountain kids like themselves. Maude came to the
camp to get Ma. She had to show Ma all the interesting craft shops
operated by the students. She was particularly taken by the
beautiful weaving and the woodworking. The boys roamed
around campus, and were more than a little attracted to the
presence of cute mountain girls.

At Berea, the battle with the mountains ended. There were
rolling hills from here to the Ohio River. So, the five-weeks' trip
continued on through Lexington, Georgetown, Corinth, Walton,
Cincinnati, and into the southwest corner of Ohio. In about
another week they would be through Hamilton, Ohio, and into
Indiana.

* * * *

Yes, Ike had remembered fatigue, but at the age of ten energy
quickly returns.

The morning paper had come. Ike wheeled over to the table at
the end of the ward, leafed through the headlines. [Jackie
Kennedy had been to Mexico for a goodwill weekend.] *Hell, she
can travel any ol' place at taxpayer expense. Big deal! I'll bet she spread lots
of good-will.*

[General DeGaulle just declared Algeria free and independent.
War is likely.] *God's sake, seems like mankind's goin' to keep on fightin'
over every little thing. Why can't people rule themselves without resulting to
crazy war? WWI sure as hell didn't solve much. It sure as hell didn't do
anything but ruin my life. All I got was a Purple Heart and seventy-five
dollars a month.*

I guess I was eager enough to be one of the expeditionary forces, but I sure as hell never expected it to be so horrible—mud, blood, noise, gore, and everyone brought to the level of animal existence. Just survive one minute at a time that was all you could do.

So, here I am seventy-two years old. Wasted! I came so close to not getting back at all. Four inches closer and it would have been my neck instead of the gas mask tube. Poor Joe Archer got my "widow maker". I got gas. Christ! I can still smell that shit. Damn! I'm just so tired. Can't get a good breath…so tired. I'd sure as hell like to go back about fifty years.

Oh, yes, I remember so well… Long hours shocking wheat, and the threshing ring. Yeah!

* * * *

Orville Parks owned the machine and the steam tractor used to drive the pulleys and belts to separate the grain and blow the straw onto a stack. There were eight to ten families in the cooperative threshing ring. Parks got his wheat harvested first, and then, each in turn would have the machine moved to his farm.

Parks would set the rig up-wind, to avoid straw and chaff blowing back onto the workers. The wagons would be in the field loading while the machinery was being set up. One man on the wagon loading and driving, two men on the ground pitching. The loader had an important job, to get the load "tied on", getting it high, and getting back to the separator without spilling. He would catch each sheaf and place it perpendicular to the sheaves just below, particularly on the outside flank of the load. Occasionally a load would be lost, and have to be unloaded enough to start the process over with another attempt to build a sound load. Some loads would reach over fifteen feet high.

Pitching was the best job. Assuming the taller men could toss the sheaves higher, they usually got that job. They could rest in the shade of the wheat shocks until another wagon came to their area to load again.

Rabbits and mice frequently hid under the shocks, while an occasional opportunistic snake could be found waiting for the unsuspecting mouse. Dude Johnson was one of the best loaders, and Ike knew he hated snakes. When one of Dude's loads was about twelve feet high, Ike scooped a black snake onto the load. As the snake cleared the edge of the load, Dude jumped off the other side. He dropped the full twelve feet and landed with a thud.

I guess I would have had the shit beat out of me had Dude not sprained his ankle.

We all had a great laugh at Dude's expense. He never let me forget that joke. He never got even, though he threatened to, almost every day.

The water boy was an important part of the team. Riding in his small buggy, he would make the rounds, dispensing water every half hour or so.

But the best part of all was the dinner. Each farm wife would host the threshing crew. All the members' wives would bring in large portions of pre-determined dishes. The meals usually consisted of three kinds of meat, mashed potatoes, egg noodles, gravy, beans, yams, sliced tomatoes, fresh bread, pickles and gallons of ice tea.

Each farm would complete the threshing operation in one day barring any breakdown in equipment. There never was a season completed without some breakdown. Everyone hoped to get his harvest done before it rained. Mr. Parks was accused of always saying just after his wheat was in the bin, "Man, a good rain now would be great for my corn."

Ike's family had ended their long journey in eastern Indiana, south of Richmond. The land was good and William had received a guarantee of being "hired on", along with his kids, to help with the cultivation and harvest. Their new house was small and modest, only slightly larger than the mountain cabin. The land in the area was not flat, but much flatter in comparison with Scott County, Virginia. They all worked the farm the first season. Walt and Joe got restless the first winter and found factory jobs which paid much better than the dollar-a-day farm wages. They had to move into a boarding house in Richmond, but they were only about eight miles away. It relieved the crowding in the small bungalow.

Those were hard times for the family, but the move to Indiana had proven to be a good choice. The land was rich and the farmers, honest and fair. There was work to do from spring plowing right on through to corn-shucking time in the fall. When fields and crops did not need plowing, there was hay to harvest, pigs to tend, and cows to milk. Farming was just a little more complex in this area. There was no tobacco to tend. The fields were larger, and the yields were at least double those from the mountain slopes...

The day of dreamy reminiscence ended early, and with the help of the nurse, he fell back onto his pillow and was soon asleep.

July 3, 1962

Ike became aware of the morning from behind his closed lids. He was on his left side. His left hand rested flat under his left cheek, his right hand tucked between his legs. He slowly opened his eyes. The orange-red light of the dawn streamed into the ward. He rolled onto his back and stared at the ceiling. Every crack in the paint was as familiar as the back of his hand. The sound of heavy breathing and snoring rose through the stale air.

An orderly came into the ward carrying his floor-mopping equipment. The smell of disinfectant from the pail soon filled the ward. Other patients slowly responded to the quiet activity.

"Get the hell outta here with that stinkin' crap."

"That shit would wake the dead."

"What the hell's goin' on. You'd think we's havin' inspection or somethin'."

"Well, we is. I be doin' whut the boss said. We is havin' the big mudda's in today, or sometime, so we's got to look spit clean. It take all day to do this wing. Sorry gent's, but I hasta start someweres. You's lucky. I be gone in a sec, and you can snooze all the damn day."

Ike figured it made little difference anyway. Just about the time you think you can take a nap, some nurse comes with a pill, probe, thermometer, needle, or piss tube to take urine specimens.

Oh Christ, do I even want to get up today?

He pushed the button to raise the head of his bed. He was so weak it was all he could do to raise his arms to feel his unshaven face. As he moved slightly, he felt heaviness in his chest, and the spasms of his morning coughing began. His chest heaved, and his throat was sore from the racking phlegm-producing episodes. After each round of spasms, his head would fall back on his pillow, and he would labor to get a healthy breath.

He felt dizzy, cold, and was covered with a clammy sweat. It was complete misery. He wondered if maybe he might have a slight fever. He would say something to the nurse when he came in.

Thoughts turned to the coming holiday and visitors who would be coming to the hospital. Would his family get over from Richmond? He hadn't seen anyone since the fall, and hadn't seen LaMoine or Bobby since lord knows when.

I guess I never did right by my boys. They sure as hell don't keep in touch with me, but then why should they? Everything I ever tried to do went sour. The damn ol' Jack Daniels and cheap wine has been my undoing. Why in the hell couldn't I stop boozen it up? I knew it was destroying all I had. I am one stupid bastard. I wish I could take it all back and try it over. Hell, I would probably make the same damn, dumb mistakes all over again.

I sure must have made life miserable for LaMoine. It was a bad mistake right from the beginning by naming him LaMoine. Has called himself "Blackie" since he was sixteen. I guess we were thinking about LaMoine Gibson. Ol' LaMoine Gibson, now there was a rounder. LaMoine Gibson was about my closest friend.

* * * *

Ike fell into a restless dream, and saw Gibby standing in front of him with his arms crossed…

"Hey, Ike, I hear there's great work out west. Let's go west and chase jackrabbits and loose women."

"Now, just how you fixin' to get there?" Ike heard himself sounding skeptical, but warming quickly to the idea.

"We could go by train."

"Train? Boy, that takes money. You got any?"

"Not much. But I've seen guys ridin' in the cars, hitchin' on free. Maybe we could get part or all the way before they threw us off. It could work. What do ya say?"

He awoke remembering the dream, which was not so much a dream as a memory. Yep, he and Gibby had done just that. What a damn fool thing to do, but what a great adventure.

Ike remembered standing in front of his Ma sayin', "Ma, me and Gib, we was talkin' bout goin' out west this summer. We hear there's good work in the wheat harvest, and besides, I need to get outta here for a spell. I need to get out on my own. I'm sixteen now and I figure I need to get a taste of more than just what's here in Richmond."

"Ike, you must be tetched in the head," Ma spat at him. "You ain't got sense God gave a frog. You go out west? That is plain dumb, boy."

"But Ma, I'm goin'…soon as I figure out how and when."

"Well, don't see as how I can stop you if your half-wit mind is set on it. But I still think yer tetched."

Next, Ike approached William. His dad was sittin' on the porch rockin' and spittin' tobacco juice over the edge of the porch. Most of it cleared the porch, but there was clear evidence of months of squirtin' and missin'. Ike sat down in the other rocker near his Pa.

"Hey, Pa, do ya know any folk who been out west?"

"Nope, guess I don't"

"Did ya ever think ya would like to go out thar?"

"Nope, guess not."

"I heard ol' Dude Johnson say they got farms out there you can't see across. An the land's so flat you can see a piss ant five miles away."

"What's on your mind, Ike? You got somthin' stirrin'?"

"Well, me and Gib, we is headin' out there soon as we can get plans made."

"That right?"

"Yep, we is goin'."

"Damn dumbest thing I ever did hear. You plumb lost your mind. You gonna just leave us? Just like that?"

"Yep, we is goin'."

"Well, if that don't beat all?" William sat back, leaned his head 'ginst' the back of the rocker and frowned.

That was the "okay" Ike had needed. Next day he ran over to Gib's house to report that he was ready to go as soon as they thought it would be right….

Ike remembered so clearly….

He had a clear memory of the dream, but it wasn't a dream as much as clear recall. That is the way it was as best he could remember. And, they had gone. Damn, that was some trip. He thought back again to the wonderful adventure…

I see us now: we're walkin, unconcerned like, at the edge of the assembly yard at the side of the train…

* * * *

The Pennsy Railroad came in from the east and left Richmond headed for St. Louis. Trains stopped regularly at the assembly yard. A large "round house" and repairs shop sat north of the "yard". They heard a train begin its slow, smoke-blowing, puffing start. The drive wheels would spin, and sand would be dropped on the track in front of the wheels, and slowly the train would gain momentum. Just as the train began to move, Ike hoisted Gib up through the door, and then Gib turned around and pulled Ike up beside him. They stood up in the middle of the boxcar and rocked with the slow, rolling motion as it gained speed. They were sure they had not been seen, since the yard was so crowded with cars, and neither the caboose or the engine was visible around the slight curve in the track.

They stood briefly, looking out the door. They turned to settle down at one end of the car to wait. Each had a bundle of personal gear, a change of clothes and some fruit. Each had a little money, but knew it was not enough to pay passage, and still have much to spend on food.

As they started toward the back of the car, they were startled to heard a voice.

"Howdy men."

They saw a man sitting in the back of the car wearing a dirty felt hat. His face sported a fine long beard, and his clean white teeth sparkled through the hair as he smiled.

"Well, where ya headed fer men?"

Ike and Gib said, "Howdy."

"We're headin' west to work the harvest,—If we can get there", Gib was quick to explain.

"My name's Zack. What be your names?"

After introductions were over, Ike and Gib settled down on the hard floor and rocked with the rolling rhythm of the moving car.

Zack broke the lengthy silence. "First time away from home?"

"Yep"

"First time ridin' the rails?"

"Yep"

"It's not the first time for me. I been travelin' up from Virginia for a couple days now. I'm headin' for St. Louis. Got family there."

"I'm from Virginia," Ike said.

"That a fact? Where be your county?"

"Family lived in Scott County, near Hilton Station." Ike explained.

"I came from over round Norfolk." Zack seemed interested in his fellow Virginian.

Ike said, "We came up about six years ago, I reckon. We walked up over the Cumberland Gap. Folks settled down here in Richmond. Most have found good work, but I got wander-bug in my pants. I can't stay round here no more. I gotta see more and try my wings."

"We hear they need men to work the harvest out west, so we want to try our hand at that at least for this summer." Gib sounded enthusiastic and sure of their success.

As Ike recalled, that was a butt-wearing trip like riding in the wagon had been coming across the mountains. By late night, after a few more water stops, the train began slowing as it entered the large train yard in St. Louis. They had seen the Great Mississippi while standing at the door. They looked at the passing scenery and also for the line detectives, or yard personnel to avoid.

Zack dropped off the train and disappeared under a stopped car. They were alone again and realized they were running low on food and water, but they could not get off yet for fear of being seen. The train was in the yard for over two hours. There was much bumping around as the train dropped cars, and attached new ones. They thought about a hot bath and some hot food, but stayed on as the train started to move again. They did not know how long it would take to reach Kansas City, so they decided one would sleep and the other would stay awake to avoid missing their next stop. But, they both slept until awakened by the jarring made as the train slowed. The outskirts of a town showed outside the partially opened door which meant they were possibly entering their destination town.

Wheat fields and corn fields had been the only crops seen for miles. The wheat was just beginning to put on its golden hue. Ike knew the crop would be about ready to cut just a few miles south. As the train pulled onto a siding, it came to a gut-jarring stop— just about dropping the guys to their knees. A sign read, "Kansas City". They quickly jumped from the box car and walked across the tracks, ducking under and between train cars until they were clear of the tracks.

They walked west along the tracks to the nearest crossing. Looking south and north, they saw no signs for food or lodging. They decided to walk north and came to a street intersection just as a man dressed in his farm coveralls and straw hat stopped his horse-drawn wagon.

Ike hailed him with a raised hand and inquired, "Where can we get some grub and a bath?"

"Looks like you boys been a travelin' right smart." The kindly face beamed down at them.

"Seems like we been movin' too fast too long," said Gib.

"We come out here to try to work the wheat. We hear there's operators out here takin' on a right smart bunch of workers. Know where we can go to find out about work?" Gib always was on the right foot ready to go.

"I just might be able to help. Climb in back. I know where we can eat and talk.

"The farmer's name was Claude Richards. He was driving a beautiful matched pair of roan mares that looked and stepped as lively as parade horses.

Not far up the unpaved street, Claude pulled the team up to the curb-side hitching post, stepped on the rim of the wagon wheel and vaulted off. Ike and Gib were quick to follow suit.

Six tables graced the front of the cafe. A long counter separated the rest of the cafe. The smell of coffee filled the air. Several men dressed in farm stained coveralls sat around one table drinking coffee, engaged in animated conversation.

Claude approached the table and shook hands with some of the men. Ike and Gib stood, not being sure what was expected of them. Claude turned to them, smiled, and said, "Have a seat at that table boys. Order what ever you want. I'm payin'."

The waitress, dressed in a neat white pinafore, wore her hair in a short-cropped bob. She wore too much make-up, but her countenance was open and friendly. She took their order of steak and eggs, toast, and coffee. The coffee, brought first, was like a tonic for their tired bodies. The steak and eggs tasted like the best food in the world and was soon consumed by the hungry pair.

The men at the table were soon finished with their coffee and conversation. They ambled out of the cafe to begin their day's work. Claude, and the man he had first approached, came over and sat with Ike and Gib.

"Name's Byron Morgan. Where you boys from?"

"Richmond, Indiana."

"Ain't in trouble with the law are ya?"

"Nope! Never!"

"How did ya get out here this early in the morning?" although he knew full well their mode of travel.

Ike said, "We came in on the morning freight."

"Kinda risky I'd say. Have any trouble?" He eyed the boys for their reaction.

"We was careful. We met some other fella goin' the same way. But we need to find work out here and we didn't have the money or time to earn train fare, if we wanted to get out here in time for the harvest. We want to work real bad."

"You boys know anything about workin' a harvest? It is hard, hot and tirin'."

Ike said, "I been workin' at farm work since I was a little tad back in Virginia. I been workin' all kinds of farm work since we moved to Indiana, and I worked the wheat harvest each year the last five years. Yes, sir, I know about wheat harvestin'."

Gib said, "I been workin' wheat harvest ever since I started out as a water boy about six years ago. Worked most all the jobs except runnin' the tractor and the separator."

"Do ya know anyone lookin' for harvest hands?" Ike asked.

"Sure do. I could use a couple sturdy boys on my crew. Pay a dollar a day to start, and expect a full day's work. You boys interested?"

"You bet!" Ike said as he stood up, practically bounding out of the chair.

"Hell Yes!" blurted Gib.

Both boys were on their feet and ready to go to work after that great breakfast.

"Well, I have a few things to do here in town before I take the afternoon train west. You can tag along or just nose around town until about one, when the train comes in. I can meet you down at the station house. We'll head out for my spread. You can pay me back for the train fare out of your first week's pay. Okay?"

Ike didn't want to butt into Mr. Morgan's business. He looked at Gib, but Gib just shrugged his shoulders. "I guess we'll just nose around a bit. If that's Okay."

They both shook Mr. Richard's hand and thanked him for breakfast and for helping them find work so quickly.

He patted them on the back and said, "You boys do good work now. I am glad it has worked out for you."

They walked around town, stayed near the train station, and made sure they were at the station when the train came in. Mr. Morgan came to the station a few minutes after the boys had settled onto the hard, waiting bench, which resembled a church pew.

The train ride ended after sundown at Hayes, Kansas. They

walked to the livery stable, waited while the horse was hitched to the surrey, and rode for an hour to get to Mr. Morgan's farm.

Ike thought of how lucky they had been to fall into the job by a chance meeting with Mr. Richards. Mr. Morgan seemed like an honest, hard-working man. Ike liked him and felt comfortable in his presence.

So, had begun his western adventure—propelling him along in a race to nowhere in particular.

His thoughts were rich with memories. *This old body had legs then, and by God, they sure did lots of walking*... He could see himself standing in the wind-blown plain with shocks of wheat stretched in front of him for over a mile. It was one of those days again— blue-black sky overhead, perpetual horizon, browned by the blowing dust. They had been shocking wheat for ever, it seemed. They were hot and tired. The temperature had risen quickly during the day; and by this time at midday, the heat was at its worst. They would have been covered with sweat-soaked clothing if they were working in Indiana; but the air was so dry here, it evaporated right away.

Thunder clouds were beginning to form on the western horizon. He could see them growing if he stood still and watched. He was always surprised by the speed with which they became full blown thunderheads with the accompanying rain squalls.

The water boy pulled up to them on his buckboard. He offered them the water jug, which they eagerly accepted. "Get on gents, dinner is about ready. I want to get to the barn before it rains."

Ike had a question about that statement, for the only cloud he saw seemed to be miles away to the southwest. But Jimmy Morgan, the youngest member of the family, was right. As they rode along on the back end of buckboard, Ike watched the sky in amazement. Cottonball puffs of cloud quickly formed almost overhead. They grew together and boiled in a beautiful dance on the hot, rising air. Within thirty minutes they were clearly forming a thunderhead climbing miles into the once clear, cloudless expanse.

The sun was soon blanketed from sight, lightning sparked in the darkening mass, and new winds began out of what had, only moments before, been a strange, unusual calmness.

Jim prodded the horse into a trot, but they never made it to the barn in time. Following a huge lightning strike about a mile west, large, smarting, rain drops slammed into their tired hot bodies. They couldn't stop to take shelter under the buckboard, for the horse was headed for the barn at more than a trot now. He would not stand still to allow anyone to get under the wagon. He had the barn and food in mind, and a horse with that mind set is as hard to stop as a mad elephant.

Riding in a steel-rimmed buckboard in an open field, in the height of a thunder storm, was not a good situation. There was nothing to do but let the horse run and hold on to in the wagon to keep from being bounced out.

Wet and laughing as they dashed into the barn yard, the boys jumped off the buckboard, helped unhitch the horse, and ran into the wide-open barn doors. They stood watching sheets of rain slam into the pools of mud. They were amazed at how quickly the storm had formed right over their heads.

Ike had never seen storms form like this. He saw many such storms during the few weeks in the plains. Back in his farmland, the storms almost always rolled in from the west behind a healthy rolling scud. But out here, they just seemed to form. A clear morning could quickly turn into a raging storm, including tornadoes. He remembered two he had seen at a distance, as they snaked across the plain, pulling dust, grass, and wheat shocks into their vortex. It had been an awesome sight.

As in Indiana, the farmers always feared the loss of their wheat harvest from untimely rains. It would take several days of rain before the shocked and piled sheaves would be destroyed. The most that would happen was a loss of half a day's work. Early the next morning, the engineer would stoke the coals in the steam engine firepit. There was adequate water was in the boiler to make steam, in order to power the wheels driving the belts powering the separator. It would take over an hour to build the pressure needed to drive the piston. But, that would come later. Now was the task of getting the wheat shocked in the field—the massive field that went on forever.

Harvest time came. The equipment was readied. The first grain to be harvested, of course, was Morgan's. The operation was much like it had been in Indiana, except for the greater distance the grain had to be hauled to get to the separator. The separator would have to be moved to several locations to eliminate those long, time-consuming trips.

The "water monkey" had an important and difficult job largely because of the long haul frequently needed to bring water to the boiler. Often, the water wagon (a huge wooden tank on wheels) would be pulled to the nearest water source, filled with water and returned before the boiler water got too low. When the water got low, the engineer would sound a whistle as a warning. Failure to get the water back in time could cause half a day shutdown. It was embarrassing for the "water monkey", and could cost him his days wages of three dollars.

As the water was heating, Ike and the loading crews were in the field loading wagons. The best timing was having the first wagon back to the separator just as the engine achieved full power. The sheaves could be thrown onto the conveyor directly from the wagon. In some operations, the sheaves were piled in huge stacks by which the separator would be parked; and the operation would require the sheaves to be pitched into the conveyor from the ground.

The separated wheat fell through wire mesh screen into the bottom collection trough. Augers then lifted the wheat into a measuring bin which held one half bushel of wheat. Careful count was kept by the separator tender, since the machinery owner was paid five cents per bushel when harvesting the wheat for others. On a good day, Mr. Morgan could make as much as forty dollars.

Mr. Morgan would ride on ahead before the threshing was finished on one job. He would arrive at the next job site a day or so ahead, making all the necessary arrangements with that grower as to the expected time of arrival. The setup of the equipment, arrangement for housing the workers, meals, and other details made for a smooth, rapid operation once the full crew was on the property.

As Ike remembered, he could not believe the size of those farms. The smallest spread worked was a square section, which was one mile on each side. Most spreads were from three to five sections. Ike felt he had walked every mile twice over as he and Gib followed the progress of the ripening grain northward.

For the most part, he walked, but occasionally he would get

rides on wagons to the next town. Upon leaving one crew manager, they would join up with another, and the hot dusty windy job would continue, as it had before, with little variation. Ike guessed he had sweat a ton of water in those few weeks.

There were fun times during the summer. The best was the circus. It came to Hayes, Kansas, one Saturday morning. They had been working a job about four miles west. The Morgan family was excited about seeing the circus, and Ike and Gib gladly accepted the farmer's invitation to ride into town with them. With an early start, they were able to find a place along the main street before the circus parade rolled by.

Ike had been to one circus in his life. The circus band led the parade. They were riding on top of a red, highly decorative wagon, the sides of which were covered with circus art of circus animals and clowns. The band was riding at least ten feet in the air, playing lively circus music. Following the band, was a large group of people dressed in tights and flowing capes. Wagons loaded with lions, tigers, bears and various wild animals, drew excited comments from the assembled throng. Then came several camels and zebras, each led by an attendant. Exclamations rose as the line of elephants came into view. Each elephant grasped the tail of the one just ahead, and they ambled softly down the dirt-packed street. An elephant tender, carrying a long pole with a metal hook on the end, led the elephants. The hook was placed gently behind the elephant's trunk to lead its lumbering, soft-footed progress. Each elephant's head was adorned with a large leather harness grasped by a beautiful woman who rode straddling the elephant's neck, with her knees tucked firmly behind the elephant's ears

Behind the elephants came a riotous phalanx of clowns who

were beating each other and chasing around, throwing candy to the crowd along the route. The last two clowns were essential. One pushed a wheel barrow; the other scooped horse and elephant manure.

The first performance of the circus was one-thirty P.M. In the time before the performance, Ike and Gib walked around the circus ground observing everything. Ike was impressed with the efficient work of the roustabouts. Most of the tents had been erected earlier in the morning, but some work was still being done before show time. The stake driving operation caught Ike's eye. One man would secure the tent rope over a stake lightly driven into the ground. Eight men with large mallets began a brief hammering, each man striking the stake in rotation. After about three rotations around the hammering circle, final tension was given to the rope around the secured stake. It was so routine and so efficient, Ike watched them work for a long time.

He watched the animal handlers and trainers feed and care for the menagerie. He was fascinated by the big cats. Up close, the lions appeared to be covered with a rich, healthy fur that highlighted the rippling muscles inside. He watched and remembered the fine animals he cared for on the farm. How different could a zebra be from an ornery mule?

In late summer, they had worked the harvest as far as North Dakota, and had experienced all the wheat harvest they could take. They arrived back in Richmond on the "Pennsy Line" only a little better financially than when they left. They were brown and lean, hardened from the weeks of constant walking in the fields.

Gib said, "The only wheat I ever want to see again is in a slice of bread." But, Ike remembered, Gib had, much later, become an Indiana farmer. He had been killed by lightning while riding on his tractor in the field.

Hell, that coulda happened to us back in Kansas for that matter. Strange ain't it?

* * * *

He was drawn back to the present by his bed neighbor's invitation.

"Come on Ike, let's get the cards warmed up. I need a good game of euchre. Take my mind off this damn ache in my legs"

Dunkin rolled his wheel chair over to the end of the ward where two other vets sat at the small metal table. Slower, and with great effort, Ike rolled over to the table. Frequent coughing spells slowed his progress.

Cards were dealt. The game moved on. So did the morning hours. Inspection of the ward was due at any time, but the players didn't give a damn. They had hated inspection while in the service, and they could see no reason to feel differently now.

Ike was weak, beads of perspiration appeared on his brow. He felt a familiar heaviness in his chest. Probably just tired muscles from all the coughing. *My fever must be gone, or else I wouldn't be sweatin'.*

"Boys, I ain't worth two spoons of spit. I'm just too damned tired. Maybe I'll whup your asses tomorrow." He slowly backed his wheels from the card table and rolled to his bedside. His head bent forward slowly and he slept a deep, restful slumber, freeing his pain and loneliness.

He missed the formal inspection team—always sharp in their full parade dress uniforms. When they appeared at the door, some idiot yelled attention, which got about as much action from the guys as a cow patty. The team moved quickly around the ward, spoke to no one, and quickly wobbled their fat administrative asses out into the polished hall, and were on their way to complete their obligatory rounds for this holiday-eve government ritual.

The nurse tapped Ike on the shoulder. "You Okay Ike?"

"Ah. yeah. just feel pretty weak. Must be gettin' old."

"Well, supper is coming. You want to eat at the table or in bed?"

"Guess I'll get in bed. You ready to give me some help?"

"Sure can. Here, let me just lift you in. Grab hold.Here we go."

With that, he lifted Ike's frail body and gently positioned him on the bed, raising the head to accommodate his need for the arriving food. Ike wanted to eat but wondered if he had the strength to get the food to his mouth. He'd be damned before he would let someone feed him. He knew, in the fringes of his mind, he was not far from being helpless. He would fight it as long as he could.

The evening meal arrived on the filing cabinet rolling cart. Each meal filed away for its designated gourmet. The meat-loaf was dry and underseasoned, the mashed potatoes and gravy were somewhat better, the green beans needed a good chunk of pork belly to make them really good, and there was the forever-present Jello. A few bites of each was all he could manage before he slumped back onto his pillow and stared at the cracked ceiling. Before night fall, he was in a sound sleep.

His chest rose and fell with the labored breathing of his scarred lungs.

July 4, 1962

The dream lingered as a dark mist in the recess of his fatigue and pain. He was awake, but the dream was a faint memory of fear bordering on panic. It must have been the impending celebration of this holiday, which was often avoided, since the trauma of the fireworks displays brought on his inner panic. The memory of HELL experienced in the trenches of France were too vividly recalled. The visual memory, though still present when called up, was overpowering with remembered terror and helplessness, and of artillery bombardments and counter bombardments during the day and long into the night.

Certainly this celebration was to be avoided as it related to the fireworks displays. This year, he would not be present. There were years when any excuse would be used to avoid going to Roosevelt Hill in Richmond and sitting with the family, listening to the exploding bombs, suffering uncontrolled tremors to the point of wanting to run and yell was embarrassing.

Something about the dream recalled this terror. He was covered with sweat. The racking cough began before he raised his head from the pillow. His metal bed frame shook from the rhythmic coughing pattern.

All his ward mates appeared to be stirring in their various stages of waking. All were confined to wheel chairs when not in bed, most had suffered their infirmity from land mines. A couple patients in this ward were nothing more than head and torso. All were younger. They seldom called him Pop just Ike, mostly. He usually enjoyed the casual banter, but there was little news to talk about except sports and the current news.

Ike reached for his bedside button. He was going to need help this morning, for he was too weak to get to the bath room. His bladder was bursting. His chest ached. His legs ached. His arms were as jelly sticks.

The nurse walked in, smiled at Ike, and said, "What's up Ike? Havin' problems?"

"Yeah, Mack, I need the urinal right now, or I'll be floatin' outta here."

"Well, let's get to the 'head' then."

"No. Not this mornin', I just don't feel like I want to move."

"Okay. But, just for now. In a few minutes I'll come to thump your back. Maybe we can help get some of that shit up out of your lungs."

Mack placed the urinal in position, covered Ike, and made cursory stops at all the other beds, chatting with each patient for a few seconds.

Ike said, "Okay, Mack, get this urinal out of here before it spills all over me."

"Yeah, Ike, it wouldn't take but a cupfull to float you outta here as skinny as you are." He took the urinal, walked to the "john" and dumped it.

When he returned, he rolled Ike onto his left side and firmly thumped him on the back. Ike's cough continued with increasing effort, but finally, large clumps of phlegm were released, which Ike spat into the bedside spittle dish.

After about five minutes of this therapy, his breathing became easier. He felt less light-headed, and his coughing subsided. He was rolled back on his back, and with the nurse's aid in adjusting his shoulders and pillow, he felt he was somewhat better. But he was weak as a kitten.

With an exhausted sigh, he let his head fall into his pillow, reached for his bed control button and raised the head of his bed. He could see all the other men in the ward in various states of waking. He felt certain they were not much different from himself. He could not deny his feeling of embarrassment about the terror lodged in the recesses of his mind. He hated the physical manifestation it produced when it emerged from its cloud bank to rain on him with damning fury, but he felt sure each of his ward dwellers had the same horrific feelings.

Each bed was a universe housing the man and his terror, a terror unspeakably ghoulish, unbelievably insane, unleashed by nations on its youths to protect or expand some territory, or preserve some unproven ideal.

The young mind has never been prepared to accept the slaughter. The basic training with loaded guns on the rifle range, the tossing of hand grenades, the thrusting of bayonets into straw filled dummies, the blasts of artillery that would wither your guts and leave your ears ringing, the yelling insults from the loud-mouth illiterate drill sergeant—none of this could prepare them. No attempt to dehumanize them into brain-washed puppets, willing to respond to any insane command, was able to prepare them for the unspeakable carnage. Each man in the room had been a victim of this madness, and his exterior disfigurement was only on a par with the chaos within.

Nightmares, sweating, uncontrolled shaking, visions of dismembered buddies, the smell of smoke and excrement and blood and gas drives each man to the brink of insanity, in order to escape the continuing reality of unbearable slaughter. There is no place to hide. Drugs, from alcohol to morphine, offered some respite from the horror; but it would re-appear out of the recesses when least wanted, leaving them weak and vulnerable.

Something in the night had triggered this terror again—something in the remembering of his family, of past Independence Day celebrations, of his loathing of the sky bombs. How much of his life had he wasted and spilled trying to wash away the horror?

His life had been promising as a youth. He was healthy and conditioned. He was a joyous, friendly youth with lots of buddies. He had enjoyed singing with his brothers. They had been singing together for years, and their blending was better than most. He remembered how excited he was when the first automobiles began to appear.

Then, the news of war in Europe became a frequent conversation topic. In November 1916, he decided, "What the hell! Might as well join the army. That would be something interesting to do." Several young men from Richmond had joined up; so, on December 6, 1916, he was inducted and found himself in uniform.

In his early years as a boy on the farm, he had learned to use a rifle and shotgun. Hunting was a frequent year-round sport and necessity. They skinned and ate all they killed if it was eatable. He remembered being a skilled marksman, hunting with a 22 caliber rifle or a 12 gauge shot gun most of the time. The challenge was to find a rabbit hunkered down in the grass and shoot him through the head but avoiding damage to the eatable meat. At times he would sit under a tree, during the early morning, propped up against the trunk waiting for a squirrel to walk along the high branches. The aim was to kill one by a shot to the head.

Marksmanship was a talent carried with him to the army, earning him a marksman medal very quickly. His affable, relaxed in manner, and his hardened condition made the training fairly easy, as he remembered it. He was given promotion to corporal rather quickly. But his familiarity with guns did not prepare him for carnage. He knew he was a lover, not a warrior. He would also have to lead his men into the trenches. He did not want this job.

He hated the huns, the FROGS, the lymies (friend and foe alike), for the stupid war that cost so much in lost life—those killed, and the living who could not put it in their past. It was always there, just on the edge of consciousness, coming into full agony at inappropriate times.

* * * *

He could not recall the dream (maybe it was not a dream), but the chill and the dread was undeniable *Well, it don't really matter. Here is where I am, and I guess this is where I stay, for awhile at least. But this is next to unbearable.*

Why do I feel this inner panic? Can't I face the past and the little future I have left?

I guess this 'Day of Independence' has hit me hard this year. I am proud I could be of service to my country, and proud that I was willing to lead some of my men through the hell, but still...it has been one continuous haunting. My "good legs" took a beating again during the war. Hell, they were pretty good to me as I look back on it. The silly marching on the parade ground day after day, the slopping through mud in France....

* * * *

Ike was quick to recall the early days in training camp—the train ride to New York, and the embarkation to France on a German merchant ship. Several German ships had been captured, or commandeered, while in American ports, after the declaration of war. Later they were used to transport troops to France.

His first sailing experience wasn't too bad for a mountain boy. The second day out under moderate swells he began to feel some nausea and was decidedly weak, but a few hours on deck watching the convoy helped him forget his uneasiness. Four troop ships were in the main body of the fleet, flanked on either side by heavy cruisers. Smaller destroyers were leading the convoy and running interference on the perimeter.

Spartan living conditions had been hurriedly constructed with bunks, four deep, along all the bulkheads; while hammocks were strung from stanchions bolted in the deck. "Head" facilities were inadequate for the hundreds of men on board. The air was stale and redolent with human sweat.

On the third day out, during morning muster, the commanding officer made a formal announcement. "Men, we are sailing to France and will land at Brest on the west coast. New railroad lines have been built. We will be transported by train as quickly as our troops are assembled. We will advance easterly toward Germany and our 'Hun' hunting ground." A boisterous roar rose from the throats of the eager young warriors for whom the horrors of conflict had not yet been revealed.

The sail must have taken about ten days. Ike was not sure at this point. All the days were spent being herded around, keeping track of the men in his platoon, gathering supplies, running over survival drills in the use of gas masks. They practiced procedures of taking cover in the trench, or charging from the trench— anything to keep the men busy and out of trouble as his sergeant ordered. "Corporal, keep these men busy."

After the arrival in Brest, the platoon was loaded into trucks and moved to a French military base. There was always the problem of someone going AWOL with the curious French ladies who were ever present near the camp gates. The French greeted these eager, cocky, Yanks like royalty. No great problems arose and the men were eager to face hell. It was like a game, and we were there to win. Liberty was granted freely during the staging period. Ike, and his men, were not slow to take advantage of the good French wine and cognac. They always returned to camp roaring drunk. The French "ladies" were quite different from most of the women they had known back home. One of the biggest surprises was the French casualness about public urination. Ike said to one of his men, when back in camp,"Hell Fire!" Ol' Mademoiselle just said "Me pissy e c", dropped her drawers and pissed right there in the gutter. Christ, I never expected to see nothin' like that." All the men related their weird exper iences as they learned about this new culture.

They were treated with a welcome beyond anything they could ever have imagined. Everywhere, citizens offered them hospitality, drinks, their homes, their bodies.

Officers frequently called assemblies to lay out the campaign lying ahead. The American Expeditionary Forces separate from the Allied command would be assigned the southern sector of the battle line from Verdun to Belfort near the Swiss Border. The maps, laid out to show their area of hell, meant very little to them. They had to go where they were told anyway. It was the camaraderie and trust in one another, which bound them together, and circumscribed the boundary of their world.

It was late in February. The weather was agreeably warm near the Bay of Biscay, but cold and wet when they unloaded from the train somewhere east of Paris. By March fifth they found themselves miserably ensconced in trenches. The bottom of the trench was muddy from the previous day's rain. Good-natured banter and bragging could be heard up and down the length of the trench, which ran for several hundred yards left and right from their position.

As evening fell, they received notice, a welcome, if you will, as their first taste of hell came with the thorough shelling. You can never outlive the memory of the explosion of that first shell. You know you are at the whim of chance when the concussion strikes with the impact of a truck, making you feel weak, helpless, vulnerable. The trench became deathly quiet, as bodies were pressed hard against the side of the trench as near the bottom as one could get. The smell of fear and human excrement was apparent. No one made comment. Each man absorbed in his fear and dread, managed his emotional control as best he could.

Was this the core of the sublimated panic? Was this, and the bloody days which followed, the filth which corroded his self control, and drove his need for solace to help him face the memory? Now, without legs, he again felt the vulnerability, the helplessness, and the fear of not being in control. With no access to alcohol he lacked and missed his crutch which so often gave him false courage or deadening of pain.

Again he thought of the fatigue through which his legs had carried him. A memory of the big side step early in the campaign in Europe swept in...

The huns were betting on breaking the back of the French forces along the Marne River. The Russians had collapsed on the eastern front. The Germans were able to concentrate their efforts on the west. At this time all allied forces were under the command of General Foch. Germans were aware of the French forces' mutiny in the spring of 1917. They were aware of heavy French losses and the condition of the French troops. A concerted frontal attack against the French could get the Germans through their defenses at the Marne. They reached the Marne on March 30th, and were determined to push through.

But on March 28th, word came down from Pershing to pull out. The Lieutenant came up to Ike's sergeant.

"Sergeant get your men out of here fast. Fall in on the road with all your gear prepared to make due haste."

"Yes sir. Are we pulling out?"

"I don't know soldier, but I think we are needed to reinforce the French lines. I'm not sure. Just get your men out now. Let's go!"

"Okay, fifth platoon! Get all your gear. Fall out and assemble on the road."

In five minutes, the fifth platoon and thousands of other Yanks were heading north.

All along the line of march, officers were hurrying the cadence, stepping out at four miles per hour. Trucks with gear and some personnel, tanks, caissons, cannon rolled by pushing the infantry to the road side.

"Move it out! Move it out! There is no sleep tonight Yanks!"

Ike, marching next to his men, could sense the urgency of this move. He did not know the full import of this action, but by its size he knew something important was in the planning. It was clear they were needed and in a hurry. Soon they were picked up by troop trucks and crammed in. They moved north on bumpy roads as quickly as the traffic would allow.

Surely this would be their initiation into glory of another hell. The platoon passed through villages on their way toward Somme. They broke from the road, unloaded, and found they were walking through fields strewn with discarded military equipment. There were large holes, and a few standing trees which seemed to have been stripped of most limbs. Presently, they were directed to a system of trenches dug along a ridge overlooking a broad valley. All gear was moved into the trench complex and the bunkers spaced at irregular intervals along the trench system.

Behind them was a row of new French cannons, on which some of the American Forces had been recently trained. Ike had heard they could fire more rapidly than any other presently used in the war. The recoil was absorbed by large hydraulic pistons. The barrel would return, after firing, to the same position. The cannon did not have to be repositioned after each firing. This allowed greater accuracy and speed. But, who could tell if they would be used this day?

Everyone had sore, tired feet. Some of the men had assumed fetal position rolled up leaning against the wall of the trench, and some were, more or less dozing, in spite of the excitement of the moment. Ike was looking east over the edge of the trench and noticed a faint pale light beginning to show on the horizon, as dawn was near.

At that moment Ike saw several brilliant flashes of fire from the plain a few miles to the east. It could only be the muzzle flash from heavy artillery. In a few seconds his assumption was born out as projectiles exploded in the valley before them. The Huns were starting a pulverizing bombardment preliminary to their frontal attack. The range of their fire was gradually increased and the shells were dropping closer. Within ten minutes their location was receiving severe pounding.

Ike looked at his men on either side hunched down trying to crawl inside themselves to become as small as possible. Each jarring explosion filled them with terror and rage.

"Check your mask! Check your mask!" Ike passed the word along to his men.

Each man quickly checked the straps and tubes of his mask. An airtight seal was essential to avoid the effects of any poison gas, which may be used. Each side in the conflict had already used mustard gas. The first reported use was by the British forces in Belgium, in September 1917. Since then, its use was common.

Wind direction was crucial in the decision to use gas as it could wreak havoc to either side. Prevailing westerly wind did not work to the Hun's advantage on this morning.

There was nothing to do but sit it out and hope you would not suffer a direct hit by the bombardment. Shrapnel protection was afforded by being positioned below ground level, but some projectiles were timed to explode in the air above the men. From the cries of pain along the line it was clearly evident that not everyone was protected. It was utter helplessness having your health and life itself so dependent on dumb chance.

Here they were waiting out their call to death or mutilation from some poor sucker a few miles away, who was manning his equipment of destruction not knowing or caring about the destruction wrought on man and property. He knew only, it was either me or them. The war, having been decided by those housed in palatial grandeur, was left to the poor sucker in the mud and blood to support and execute it. Now, in this modern war, one did not face his so called enemy face to face, but pointed weapons from miles away, to rain down lethal showers of metal.

From behind, Ike heard the roar of the French three-inchers, as they began their answering horror. His ears rang and his head ached from the continued explosions. The men in the trench could not know the outcome of such bombardment, but as the morning light exposed the surrounding scene, the aftermath was a scarred desolate landscape.

Ike hazarded a quick look over the edge of the trench. Trees were blown down, shattered in two, devoid of limbs. No decent spring foliage would be likely in this area. How he would have welcomed the sight and aroma of the beautiful mountain laurel of his Virginia home. The ground was pulverized, pock-marked, with little or no grass after the two hours of bombardment laid down by the Huns.

The German bombardment stopped, but the American manned French three-inchers still pounded away. Their target had shifted from the German artillery to the area about two miles ahead across the low valley in front of them. Out of the trees, foot soldiers and tanks could be seen advancing across the broad expanse. The battle was joined. The artillery was laying down a barrage within the approaching wave of flesh and metal.

About the middle of March, new Browning automatic machine guns and rifles appeared on the line—recent shipments having been rushed from Browning to the front as quickly as possible. The men had not been checked out in this weaponry, but it was a morale builder to see and hold this new hope of survival. The guns proved to be accurate and efficient for their intended destructive purpose.

Within about thirty minutes the approaching wave was within range. Each man, resting his left elbow on the edge of the trench began to pick his target and stop the advance. The chatter of rifle and machine-gun fire was heard down the long line of defense on this ridge. The Huns were at a disadvantage in the open with no trench cover. The Yanks' artillery had disabled most of their tanks, and their advance on foot was sure suicide. They returned what damage they could, but the Yanks were proving to be good marksmen, and the advance petered out. By late afternoon, the Huns began to pull back across the low ground. Gas bombs were dropped within the retreating mass of straggling mankind. The battle of Chateau Thierry was history.

The Germans, not having expected the fresh Yank troops to be in this sector, had miscalculated the fire power to be thrown up against them. However, the Huns were still a strong force and though their advance had been thwarted this day in March 1918, they still felt they could cross the Marne and push their way into Paris.

This hun offensive at Chateau Thierry was stopped. The Hun's drive was slowed. The U.S. Third Division held Chateau Thierry. The huns did reach the Marne on March 30th, but called off the offensive. On June, 4th, U.S. forces counter attacked. Ike was on the move again. They uprooted the Germans from Vaux, Bouresches, and Belliau Wood. Ike felt like he was on the move constantly. Underfed by field rations, exhausted from lack of sleep, encouraged by the positive turn in the war, he kept on his feet and encouraged his men to keep alert.

Spring was loose in the land, but trees made devoid of foliage were unable to celebrate this season. The weather had gradually warmed since they landed in Brest. They rested more easily now, but were on the move more. And, though they had slowed the Hun's advance, the Huns kept pressing for a weak spot in the allied lines. They attacked again at Compiegne on June 9th, but their drive was halted by June 12th, as the French and American forces held.

Forces were frequently pitched together in hand-to-hand combat, slashing, shooting, and grasping each other in primal desire to survive. Advances were often made one trench line at a time. The routine: charge out, or slither out on your stomach, always trying to avoid the withering fire of the enemy's guns, over blood, body parts, equipment, and mud. This would greet the advancing warriors, just as in past wars of senseless annihilation. But, move ahead they did. Steady but difficult advances were gradually made during the summer.

All the men in Ike's platoon felt benumbed from fatigue.They needed a break. But they were still moving toward the huns, not away, as toward Paris for example. Ike saw evidence in the lack of conversation. Each man seemed withdrawn. Each man was too spent to give a damn about anything except this moment, and surviving. Ike tried to keep the morale boosted by kidding and probing his men to think of getting that long-awaited rest leave. They had been in the front line of action for five months. Ike had been appointed sergeant on June 6th, but he was not sure he wanted the increased responsibility.

He did not realize how soon he would be seeing "Pari", but circumstances were set in motion at the headquarters of General Foch. On or about the first week of July, 1918, General Foch gathered his staff around a large layout of the general battle situation. There they planned an offensive against the Marne.

The heat of summer was pouring down. It was July. Casualties had been heavy for both sides. Since March, the Germans had suffered one million casualties. On the afternoon of July 16th, the word came down. "Get ready to move out. Get your gear and equipment on the ready." In this heat Ike's men were on the move again.

When the evening "afterglow" had faded, lines of trucks began assembling loading men and equipment. Everything, from cannons to field kitchens, was loaded in. Horse drawn vehicles and trucks filled the road under the cover of darkness. The foot soldier was grateful for the ride which saved his legs, but not relishing the thoughts of death and gore to come tomorrow. Each man grimly hid the dread gnawing so painfully in his mind, and with a vacant facade, let himself be led to the slaughter.

Corporal, Joe Archer, sat next to him in the back of the truck. Joe had a this big toothy smile that lit up a broad face which sported a shaggy mustache. A mellow baritone, his voice projected self confidence and warmth. His blue eyes jumped from the cover of the black brows and mustache with a glimmer of mischievousness. The slight hint of Kentucky accent left no doubt he hailed from southern Indiana. Joe was six feet two inches tall, and weighed in at about two hundred ten. He was a good corporal, and Ike had recommended his advancement to sergeant.

On their ride Joe said, "I have a feeling this is going to be a big one."

Ike replied, "None of them are small. What do ya mean Joe?"

"I don't know, but our moving at night like this—we must have a big surprise for the Kaiser."

"It sure as hell seems that way, don't it?"

"Think we are going to get this damned war over soon?"

"God, I hope so. I don't know what's keepin' the Huns on their feet, or why they want to fight this war anyway. Hell, we ought to give them France. It would serve them right. These FROGS are crazy as crabs; always in your hair and in the way."

"Hey, Ike, I don't see you running from those chubby French mademoiselles."

"Yeah, but that's different."

"Oh sure, Yeah! You don't want to turn them over to the Huns do ya?"

"Don't figure it makes much difference either way. They know how to survive. Give them bread and wine and they will live forever. They only use us Yanks for what they can get from us, and ya can't blame 'em I reckon."

"They sure as hell been treatin' us right."

"Up to now. But I got a feelin they are throwin' us into a meat grinder on this one. That General Foch must be going for the big one. This move looks like he plans to make a big push, and I have a feelin' we are going to be right in the middle of it again."

As the troop truck came to a halt, Ike commanded. "On your feet men." He yelled above the cacophony of sound. "Fall in on the left. Stay together. We'll wait for the Captain."

The Captain came from the head of the convoy, calling platoons to move into the field by the side of the road. "Assemble your men in the field. Hurry it up. We have to move out now."

Each platoon sergeant quickly led his men to the field. All along the road the process was repeated. The tide of personnel and machinery was spilling into the field like a massive hemorrhage. New loads of men and equipment filled the road behind them and the mass of mankind spilled out of the trucks again.

The assemblage of war machine and material was such as never before used in war. This was the major leap forward in the technological ways to kill. The development of tanks and aircraft, the use of poison gas, artillery like the Huns now had with a range of seventy-five kilometers, all spoke well of man's inventiveness and madness.

The troops moved eastward across a broad and broken plain throwing planks across trenches to move across without climbing down and up the other side. They stepped over or around broken equipment and barbed wire lines, walked around shell holes ten to twelve feet across, they came to a complex of trenches. Row after row of trenches, snaking north and south, more or less, were filling with men, rifles, machine guns and ladders.

It was early morning now. Dawn would come all too soon. There came a muffled sound of moving equipment and personnel from the west, as the flow of supplies continued to arrive and disperse. The men settled into the trench as best they could.

The order came down the line to check all equipment. The new Browning automatics were broken down and thoroughly cleaned. Ammunition belts were checked again, and gas masks were checked for a snug fit. The tension was eased by raw jokes and friendly teasing, but all were secretly wondering about the day ahead.

They were soon given a prelude. The yanks' artillery began a pre-dawn bombardment into the forest ahead, but not yet in view for the troops. The continuous pounding was earth-shaking even though the guns were well west of their positions in the trenches.

The rumbling, which soon became audible, proved to be hundreds of Sherman tanks rolling east. Shaped like tilted rectangular boxes, the tread moved around the outer perimeter of the box driving the tanks along over trenches, through shell holes, across ridges, and through everything. They moved out as a driving wedge in advance of the foot troops.

The call came down the line."Move out!"... "Over the top men!"... "This is it!"..."Let's get this hell over with!"

Each man grabbed his equipment scurried up the ladder and trotted ahead, executing each trench in its turn.

Then the Huns opened up with a counter barrage, lobbing fragmentation shells and gas into the advancing ranks. Men dropped into the nearest trench for protection, and immediately donned their gas masks.

Ike's men were all together in a trench where they found some protection from shell fragments. Each man knew he was at the complete mercy of chance. Should a shell fall into or near the trench there would be no coverage to save them. Each man became as small as possible, withering inside from sheer terror.

As the bombardment subsided, Ike eased up the side of the trench to view the terrain. He rested his elbows on the edge of the trench, cradling Browning in the bend of his elbows.

Archer climbed up beside Ike and looked at the scene. "This is going to...." The shell exploded forty feet away.—Not another word came from him. The gas laden shell had served the purpose for which it was so malevolently invented.

Ike turned and saw most of Archer's neck torn away and knew his destruction had been immediate; but the turning of his head opened the hole in his gas mask tube, made by the same fragment.

Instant blindness, searing "pepper hot" burning of the skin and the lungs came on without warning. The only logical action would be flight, try to get away from the burning gas. Quickly, out of the back side of the trench, Ike stumbled to the rear, fell into the trench behind. A breath of clean air was all he needed, but there was none. He passed out.

Being in bed, seeing white walls through blurred vision, terrible pain in the nose, mouth, and lungs, other people near, all became part of his awareness like a slow motion dream. Tears streamed from his eyes. His face was on fire. But he could not get a breath of air. It was extremely painful, and it felt as if his lungs had closed down.

During the first two days after his awakening, he was in and out of this world. Gradually he became aware, that this war game was over for him. Every day the nurses came with warm, medicated water, washed his face thoroughly, and put some kind of oil in his eyes. The burning was still almost unbearable, though a little less painful than when he first arrived at this field hospital. His eye-sight was still blurred.Tears constantly filled his eyes as his system tried to wash away the poison. Coughing did not seem to give any relief. His chest felt heavy, and his lungs were still on fire. After three days, he still could feel no relief from the burning and fire-like pain.

This field hospital was filled with soldiers showing no outward sign of injury. Victims of the awful burning "mustard gas" were coming in increasing numbers from the Argonne Forest battle. Others were coming with no visible injury, but injured none the less by what was called "shell shock". Some victims suffered from both disabling conditions. It was only after a week or so of treatment that the staff could determine if the gassed victims also suffered from emotional damage.

Victims crowded the stone-walled structure. The high arched ceiling and arched windows told Ike the field hospital was housed in some part of an ancient church. The gray stone walls and the tile floors provided shelter from the August heat. In the corner of the ward stood a soldier. He stood six feet four inches at least. His broad shoulders and muscular arms suggested power and confidence. His head hung forward. His chin rested on his chest, and the powerful arms hung limp. This tall and immobile figure had stood in this catatonic state all day, responding to nothing. In the next bed from the corner, a patient had his knees pulled up to his chest, rocking back and forth like a newly wound metronome, with tears streaming down his cheeks. Next to him, strapped to a cot, a patient was wildly screaming "NO, NO, NO", trying to get free of the bonds that protected him from self injury. Ike knew not whether these men had also been gased, but it was clear they were indeed injured. He wanted to shut out the pain around him. In his mind, he felt he was in some place between the catatonic and the manic, yet he felt a sense of relief. He need not feel guilty about being away from the carnage. He didn't want to admit to the terror still churning inside, but there it was, none the less.

After he had been bathed and nursed to some state of physical stability, he was moved to a base hospital near Paris. After a few weeks he was permitted to leave. Though weak from lack of oxygen, he went with some of his fellows to see the sights of Paris. Returning to the hospital however, was always welcome. The tours were infrequent, and tiring.

On August 8th, General Haig attacked the German 18th and 2nd Armies. The Huns withdrew in a panic. General Ludenforff declared it the "Black Day of the German Army."

He heard the daily news from the front. The Huns had been put to rout. The Yanks were successfully engaging St. Mihiel, which fell, and by September 16th, was cleared. A major thrust at the Argonne Forest took place during September. The Americans cleared the Argonne Forest, and had moved on to the east and managed to cut German supply lines. By early Fall, Germany was making peace overtures.

At five o'clock A.M., on November 11th, in a railroad car in

Compaigne, the armistice was signed. Pandemonium broke loose among citizens of France. Some of the soldiers at the front just sat and wept.

He smiled as he remembered those wonderful days immediately after the signing. It was soon after, he was put on board a hospital ship bound for home. Release from the hospital was delayed due to the difficulty of his breathing. He was not confined to complete bed rest, but was kept under medical care while they tried to heal the damage to his lungs, too much damage had been done. He was told they would never be completely functional. He would suffer shortness of breath from now on.

On May 12, 1919, he was discharged from the service, at Fort Zachary Taylor, Kentucky. Isaac L. Godsey, Serial number 555301, Honorable Discharge, awarded his service bars and the Purple Heart. Rank—Sergeant.

* * * *

Light from the golden sunset gradually faded away. The overhead lights from the high ceiling in the ward came on, and the evening settled in. The day had been a catharsis for his acknowledged terror. Maybe the gas injury was only part of his disability. He knew his terror was disabling many times, and today while recalling the events of the Great War to End All War, he realized just how much shell shock was a part of his pattern. He had covered up well. It was never discussed in his family or among his veteran friends.

Ike slept through the night of July Fourth 4th, undisturbed by the bombs bursting in air. The ceremony took place at a central park in Dayton, and no sound of the aerial display reached his ward. He had had enough aerial display for his life time.

July 5, 1962

He awoke before dawn, dizzy, hot, congested, and barely able to lift his arms. He needed the urinal in the worst way, as usual. He reached his call button with effort. After a time, which seemed much too long for his bladder, the night attendant walked up to his bed.

Speaking quietly, he asked, "What d'ya need soldier?"

"Urinal."

"Right."

"I feel dizzy and hot, and weak as a sick cat. Want to check my temp?"

"Will do."

The attendant left without comment after reading the thermometer.

Ike managed a light and restless sleep for a few more hours. The sun was streaming in the east windows as he again opened his eyes on another day.

Every morning it was the same routine; clear the junk out of his lungs and gain the courage to get out of bed. He felt a familiar pang of loneliness as if in an isolated bubble where no one could touch, or speak to him.He felt he was cut off from the outside world. He knew this was not true, but the feeling lingered. He was weighed by such a feeling of distress as to bring tears to his eyes as he yearned to see his family. Why in the hell hadn't anyone come to see him during the holiday? He hadn't seen Emma, Mae, or the boys for six months.

He did not want to get out of bed this morning. The weakness he had experienced earlier was like a heavy weight on his shoulders. He could barely move his arms.

The attendant came to survey the ward and check on those early risers who were beginning to stir offering to give a lift to anyone who needed it. When he reached Ike's bed he said, "I brought you some aspirin. Your fever is above normal."

"I was pretty sure it was. How high is it?"

"It was at one hundred and two when I took it a few minutes ago. I let you sleep 'cause I was sure you needed the rest. This pill should help. We'll have the doc listen to you when he comes in a little later. Do ya want to get up now?"

"Thanks for the pill. I'll just stay in bed. Takes too damn much effort to get up."

Sleep came again and with it visions of his family as they were when he had hopes and dreams. The memories of faces, laughter and songs were fleeting. There was a red-headed little girl with flying tresses, and black-haired little boys, and a petite brown-haired woman with big brown eyes. Flashes only; but vivid reminders that came like a sudden storm which stung your face, and you couldn't look into it.

The additional hour of rest did nothing to ease his lethargy. He was awake with eyes closed. He felt the presence of the doctor just as he said, "Good morning soldier. How you feeling this morning?"

"Hell, Doc! I ain't runnin any foot races. That's for damn sure," and he smiled weakly. "But just between us old vets, I gotta say I feel like I'm sittin' on a bomb with a short fuse. My feet ache, my head aches, I'm weak as a sick flea."

The doc smiled and reached for his right wrist to take the customary pulse. Off came the stethoscope from the customary resting place around the neck. The cold membrane felt good on Ike's hot skin as the Doc placed the scope around the chest.

"Ike? Can you turn up on your side for a minute?"

With a grunt, Ike rolled onto his right side. The doc placed the scope at different places, then placed his left hand on Ike's back and thumped the middle two fingers with the finger tips of his right hand. The sound seemed dull, lacking any resonance.

"I could send you up for x-rays Ike, but I don't think that is necessary. I'd bet my right arm you have developed a little pneumonia, so I'm going to get you started on some medicine. That should take care of it. I don't need to tell you to take it easy. Don't go out and play basketball or chase the nurses. Just take it slow and easy. Do what you feel like."

"Well that won't be much. That's for sure." His resignation came through in the slow, quiet whispered response.

It was an hour before his medicine was delivered in the form of a shot in the arm.

He spent the morning in bed as immobile as stone.

The morning news came as a background noise. He felt too

exhausted to care, but still caught snatches of baseball scores and other matters of temporary importance.

* * * *

[Battle rages in Algeria following the independence granted by France…100 killed in the first hour of fighting]…*who is fighting who, and who gives a damn…the stupid zealots…what difference will it make in the end?*

[Harvard Museum Diamonds Stolen]…*big deal…Jackie should have been wearing them on her trip to Mexico…*

[Senate is in round two in their debate on price supports for US sugar producers]…*that's a pork barrel issue if I ever heard one…wonder what Senator is getting a big payoff to push that legislation?*

[Latin countries object to cut in their exports.] *they can't fight Capital Hill…*

On and on droned the news, and Ike found a few more minutes of sleep through the droning of the radio. He awoke to the sound of some good ol' country music. It brought instant recall of the fun he had with his brothers in an earlier day, when they sang a lot of the old country specials and some great spirituals. *It has been a long, long time. We sure had a melodious time of it.*

* * * *

I sure would like to see my brothers again, but that will never be, I'm sure. Sylvester was the stable one of the clan. Sylvester had married Blanche Henley and had settled into the marital life with comfort. It was good to visit with them. It was at Syl's house he first met

Emma Henley Grosse. She was a petite five feet two, with dark hair and big brown eyes that belied a spit-fire personality behind them. She was an open and cordial young divorcee with a cute red-headed five-year-old daughter. Her openness and quick wit caught his attention. Emma lived with Blanche and Sylvester while trying to get her life back together after her divorce from an alcoholic looser. She had lived in Greencastle, Indiana, but now she was living temporarily with her sister. Blanche's family was just beginning and Emma could see her presence was going to make life hard for her sister.

Ike first met her when he was home for a short leave. When he returned to camp he wrote to her, asking her to write to him and to stay in touch. This she did. Their relationship became serious, and they were married in the spring of 1919 just after his discharge in May of that year. Emma wasn't about to let this tall handsome soldier get away from her. He was fun-loving, caring, and had a unique unpredictability. They went square dancing, and did things with her daughter, Mae, included. Ike gave special attention to Mae. She had quickly won a spot in his heart. She was always on the move, and her bright eyes filled with mischief missed very little.

LaMoine was born in May 1920, and Mae took him as her special property to protect. Life looked good to Ike. He was able to get employed as a "trimmer" in a small auto manufacturing plant in Richmond. He was good at his trade. Along with the seventy-five dollars a month from the disability pension, they were able to save a little money. He was invited to join the Veterans of Foreign Wars, and the Disabled American Veterans. Emma joined the auxiliary. They made friends quickly and attended meetings regularly. Those were the good days for the family.

Ike found the bar at VFW to be a perfect place to unwind. The comrades spent long hours swapping lies, adventures, and near misses, but they never spoke of the absolute horror harbored deep in their minds begging to be forgotten.

As Ike recalled, his drinking had become more and more important to him. He would stop off at his favorite bar, located just east of the "E" Street bridge, spanning the Whitewater River. It was conveniently located on his way home from work each evening. Visits to the bar slowly began to last longer than he intended, and he was getting him home later and later for the usual dinner hour. Emma soon became angry by his "don't give a damn" attitude. Her sharp nagging tongue and spit-fire personality only made him wish she would just shut up. He was only passing a little time with the boys. What the hell was the big deal? Nag, nag, nag! That was all she knew how to do. Then he would feel guilty. He didn't want to make life more difficult for her but, hell, he wasn't hurting anybody. He'd try to cut his visits to the bar shorter and get home at a reasonable time. It never quite worked out that way. His guilt was felt, apologies given, but his behavior remained unchanged.

In August, 1927, Bob was born in their little house on Ratliff Street in Richmond. Tension eased for a couple months then Emma was hospitalized for a gall bladder removal. Soon out of the hospital with the family back together Emma renewed efforts to get the family squared away.

Work had been good, and Ike had managed to save enough money to start building a house on Ratliff Street. The size of the family called for more living space. Mae was a teenager now and needed a room of her own; and with work holding strong, the future seemed golden.

The work on the new house moved along with amateur speed, aided very little by the spectacular supervisory skills displayed by Emma. She had answers for how to cut the angles, hammer the nails, and brace the walls. Ike, not being a skilled carpenter, was filled with frustration much of the time. Her "know-it-all" instructions caused frequent outbursts from the frustrated, tired factory laborer. Ike remembered, and retold, one special encounter when he finally said to her, "Emma, just because both your brothers are cabinet makers don't mean you were born with a hammer in your ass. Get out of here and let me get some work done."

It was a time of plans and expectations, but also of growing tension. Emma was aware Ike was showing the same signs of alcoholism as her first husband. She wondered how she was so lucky to pick another alcoholic as a husband. And now she had three kids. It would be impossible to make ends meet if she were on her own. Living with his increasing addiction was almost impossible. She would have to try to get him to stop his carousing. So she nagged on and on to no avail.

As he lay in bed weak and lonely, Ike remembered all these good old days, but also could see with hindsight that he had not been in control of his drinking at any time. It had destroyed all chance he had of a normal family life—a life he would give anything to recapture. But it was too late now; the damage had been done.

I did a lot of dumb, foolish tricks. How could I have avoided all the pain and guilt? It just seemed so natural to be doing all the things my buddies were doing. It was a good time and a lousy time all at once. When I think of all the times I let some barfly help me get stone cold drunk and then steal my money, it makes me see I was lucky to have my family around for as long as it lasted. I never intended to stay in the bar for more than one cold beer. Well, maybe two.

Then after two, the conversation was so joyous. The third bottle came from out of nowhere. Someone had bought him a round. He would have to buy the next one. After that he was feeling light and good all over. There was nothing but the present, and it felt good. This was the pattern each time, but he was caught up in the habit and there was no other way to get this same kind of peace.

Blanche Godsey was on his ass all the time to come to church with her and Sylvester, get down on his knees, confess his sins, and get right with the Lord. Well, she could go to hell for all he cared. Who was she to feel so almighty perfect. He wasn't about to buy into her cheap, loud-mouth holy-roller church, with the sanctimonious, pompous, phony, loud-mouth preacher, who could preach about nothin' but sin, repentance, salvation, hell's fire and damnation. He had seen enough of hell's fire. He had turned to God in the blackest times under fire, and where was He? Whose side was He on? What did he need of religion. If it made Blanche feel good that was okay by him. But they could leave him alone. Emma wasn't having anything to do with that church either. She must have seen through the phoniness too.

* * * *

Where is He? Where is this God who is offering me salvation? I wish I could be so sure He would help me, for I sure ain't much help to myself. Seems like I have spent my life a firefly, flitting around. Sometimes I can see the light, and other times I see nothing but hopeless despair. I found my peace in the bottom of a wine bottle. My church, my fellowship, was with my generous friends at the tavern. They were my peace, my joy, my escape, and my reality check. And they let me down too. All of them proved false, just like the self-righteous holier-than-thou tongue-speakin hypocrites. So where can I turn? Is there any way to find inner peace? I guess it is too late now. My firefly existence is burning out.

I never should have married. I'm no good for settlin' down. I need to be free, to be able to be on the move, to roam the plains with no destination and goals. Marriage places the heavy gold chain around your neck—pulling you back to obligations and commitments. The few times I tried to get away from the obligations and the guilt, but the peace didn't last long enough. Every damned thing I tried to do just went to hell.

I thought for sure I could get that new house built. I would have too, if it hadn't been for the depression, the shop closing, and the whole economy going down the drain. The Bank wasn't slow about re-possessing the incomplete house. I have always known I could have finished that house, but the timing was just against me as it has always been. I guess after that everything just went to hell in a hand basket.

Farm work had always been a place where I could earn some money, but I remember, the only place I could find where the family could live was way up in Randolph County, a mile north of the cross roads general store called, "Bartonia". It wasn't much of a house, but it was shelter. But I couldn't see any future for me or the family. I was share-cropping a few acres and trying to find any work I could. There was just nothing. I was trapped; stuck up there in that God-forsaken small farm, with little or no hope for any improvement for my family. What the hell was the use? What was I going to do? Oh well, what's done is done. It doesn't make any difference now. No need even to think about it anymore. Who cares anyway. That's all in the past. I ought to get out of this bed, but I don't think I can even sit up. I feel so sleepy.

Welcome sleep came, but did not stop the brain's searching... A long train, rolling through flat country side...he was back on a freight train again. There was the familiar smell of straw bedding, and animal pungency. A great pair of gentle black eyes starred at him. He felt the calm strength, the longing...a great bulk of a body, the gentle touch from Betsie's probing quest for satisfaction; her trust in him.... The train whistle sounding through the night. He felt the urgency to be going... Vision of a huge blue and white striped canopy, mobs of people, rushing everywhere, shouting, organized mayhem. A vision of leaving the box car with Betsie following, guided only by his firm but gentle pressure on the hooked staff under her trunk. The people parting to let him pass as his beautiful lady paraded to her menagerie tent. This gentle creature, this wonder of nature, this money maker was his friend. Suddenly, family, friends, former co-workers, everyone was milling around...no place to move—no escape from what had now turned into a mob, chasing him and beating on his back...he didn't know why they were beating him...he could not escape...he ran to a large open tank and jumped into the water, as if to escape swarming bees.

He woke feeling the coolness of a wet cloth gently bathing his forehead. He was thirsty and hot. The nurse had pulled his covers down, and proceeded to bath his chest and arms.

"This can help lower your temperature. You were quite restless while sleeping."

"Yeah, I was dreamin'. Dreamin' about my friend Betsie."

"Betsie? She must have been cute."

"Well, Cute, wouldn't be a good word for her. She stood about ten feet tall, and weighed in at about four tons."

"Oh, man! You shittin' me or somethin'? You really 'sicko' my man."

"No my man, she was a great soul, with a heart as big as her bulk, and a tender, gentle touch, but she could crush you in an instant."

"No doubt, with a bulk like that. So, what's the answer to this riddle. I'm stumped."

"Betsie was a great 'Indian Elephant'. I was her caretaker for awhile when I traveled with the Hagenback & Wallace Circus."

"No foolin' man, you did that? Wow! Now that is one big dream you done had."

"One of the best times I ever had was travelin' with the circus."

"Man, you is one surprizin', crazy, dude. You was a circus man? Now don't that beat all?"

"Yeah, I joined up with the circus two different times, but this first time was a move of desperation. I had moved my family to this God-forsaken place called "Bartonia". I planted the crops, began looking for jobs in the area around Winchester and Union City. There was no work at all. I was going crazy. I had heard a circus had its winter quarters in Peru, Indiana. So, I thought 'what the hell', maybe I can find work with the circus. Always was fascinated by the circus, so why not. Never said nothin' to nobody. Just took off. Just like that. That was some experience. Traveled with them for most of two months. Probably should have discussed it with my wife, but I knew there would be hell to pay, so I just beat it."

"Well, you are full of surprises. Did you work as a clown."

"Nope, guess I was cut out to be the farmer and take care of some of the animals."

Ike eased over on his side to let the nurse bath his back with the cool damp cloth. It felt good against his feverish, parched skin. He closed his eyes trying to concentrate on the cooling effect of his bath.

"I don't feel much like it, but I guess I should get up for awhile. Just laying here ain't no better than sitting in that wheel chair. I'm ready whenever you say."

"Okay soldier. I can do."

With the chair rolled to the side of the bed, wheels locked, back adjusted, Ike was lifted into the chair.

"Where to soldier?"

"That's Okay friend. I'll roll it after awhile. I'll just sit here for a spell."

Ike was sitting facing the window and could look out on the tree-lined driveway entrance to the hospital grounds. The bath had given him some relief, but he still felt the fatigue caused by his condition. It was hard to think coherently. He was soon just letting himself think in free fall. Betsie and the circus came first to mind.

* * * *

He stood again in the circus office in Peru, Indiana. The pleasant-looking lady behind the desk looked up, smiled, and said, "What can I do for you?"

"I want to talk to somebody about working with your circus."

he said in a tired voice. He stood with his dirty workhat clutched at his side.

"Let me see what I can find out for you," the receptionist said as she swung her chair around and took a few steps behind her. She opened the wood-paneled door, and spoke softly to someone inside.

Mr. Watts, the assistant manager, emerged. His pleasant face sported a full mustache. His eyes were deep and kindly. A man of average frame but not particularly imposing. In his openfaced manner he smiled at Ike, and said, "My name's Ira Watts, of Hagenback and Wallace. And you are?"

"Ike Godsey, Mr. Watts."

"Ever work with a circus before?"

"No, sir."

"What have you been doing?"

"Well, sir, farming and factory work mostly."

"Farming you say? Like to work with animals?"

"I guess I've had to, most of my life. Regular farm animals you know."

"Well, we might be able to use someone like you. Nancy will give you a few papers to fill out for our personnel records, should we take you on. While you are doing that, I want to call one of my men to show you what we have here before we make any commitment. Okay?"

The secretary handed Ike a printed one-page form, and nodded toward the table in the corner, on which were several pencils. "Just take a seat over there Mr. Godsey, and fill out this form."

Ike had just signed the form and handed it back to the

secretary when the outside door opened and Mr. Watts came in followed by a man dressed in farm denim shirt and jeans, and dirty, cowboy boots.

"Ike, I'd like you to meet the best animal tender in the business, Cheerful Gardner. Cheerful, this is Ike Godsey. He wants to work with us. Will you please show him what we have here, and then see if you think he could help us. Okay, Ike?"

Cheerful and Ike drove across the Wabash River and followed River Road east about three miles where they reached the Mississinewa River just south of where it runs into the Wabash. They crossed the Mississinewa. The bridge exit was near the entrance of the circus wintering ground. There was a complex of three large, two-story barns, like you find on almost any farm, but the inhabitants were somewhat different. On the right side of the central drive-through were stalls filled with miniature ponies and large draft horses. On the left side, stalls contained seventeen camels and two llamas. In a large area with an oversized door to the outside stood six huge elephants each with a heavy log chain around one front foot. This was just six of the herd of twenty-nine of the huge beasts.

Ike had seen elephants in the circus, but as he stood there looking through the bars in front of the manger, he felt dwarfed.

"This is Betsie, and this is Rani," Cheerful said, pointing to two elephants in turn. "Our last caretaker for these two, and a lot more, had to leave us last week. I have had to add his work to my list of chores around here. They are gentle souls, but you always have to be alert to their moods. These ladies are eating machines. You wouldn't believe the amount of hay they can eat—or the amount of manure produced either."

The tour continued through another barn. The stalls were all barred enclosures, housing more exotic breeds including ten zebras and twenty five big cats. Only ten cats performed. The rest were used in the menagerie tent. Across the central drive, a large cage housed two polar bears and a hippopotamus. There were several open stalls filled with bales of hay and straw.

"All these critters need daily care. Feeding, visiting, doctoring, and stall cleaning." Cheerful looked at Ike as he spoke, trying to detect any reaction.

"It looks simple to me," Ike said. "I've never worked with big cats before. Can't say I feel real comfortable with them right now."

"They're pussy cats really, as long as we keep them well fed. They have never been in the wild, and their trainer has raised them from birth. But you still need to be careful when working around them. They can cause some pretty painful scratches." Cheerful kept watching Ike, and saw no negative reactions. "Anyway, you will be working mainly with the elephants, with me. I am superintendent of elephants.

They drove back to the office. Cheerful walked in with Ike. They were shown into Mr. Watts' office. Cheerful said nothing, he just nodded his head and winked at Ike.

Mr. Watts said, "Well, what do you think of my farm, Ike?"

"I didn't see any milk cows."

Both men laughed.

Mr. Watts said. "We are scheduled to start our summer tour next week. It is seven days a week for those working the animals. Travel every night unless we have an extended engagement, such as our first one. Up at dawn, unload the train, set up the show, tear down the show, load up the train, on to the next town. It's a never-ending routine. Of course, we have a system pretty well organized. Everyone knows their job. Everyone works two or more assignments, and pitches in to help anyone else when needed. We are a close-knit family. We stick together. Have I scared you off yet?"

"Nope. I'd like to give it a go, if you can use me." Ike looked Mr. Watts in the eyes and smiled.

"Okay." Watts stood and extended his hand. Their shake was firm a one pump variety.

The secretary came in and said, "Mr. Godsey, I will need some papers completed before we can get you started. Will you come with me please."

Ike turned to Watts and said, "Thank you. I'll give you my best."

Watts just nodded his head once, and smiled.

Ike was now a circus man.

Cheerful, was waiting outside when Ike finished the paper work. He motioned for Ike to join him. They drove to an area near the barns. Not quite adjacent to the barn, were situated some one-story buildings, which Ike soon discovered were housing units for currently active members of the circus family. He was shown inside, where he found a large room with bunk beds along one side, a simple cooking stove, and a table and chairs.

"Well, Ike, this will be your quarters for a few days. You won't be here long, as we start our tour in a week. Our first show is in Chicago at the Coliseum for fifteen days. In the meantime, we will keep busy tending these animals, and getting things ready for the start of this new season. The population around here will increase right smart as we get organized to load the train and head out."

"Well, I've got all I need for now—a roof, a bed, and hopefully something to eat."

"The mess hall is next door. They will sound a bell when it's meal time."

And so, Ike remembered his first contact with some of those who would quickly become like family for him in a short time. He was soon to get his introduction to the care and feeding, and feeding, and feeding of Betsie, Rani, and their herd. Cheerful had proven to be a reliable boss and sidekick. They worked well together, finding they had much in common. Both were running from bland nothingness of their present lives. Both had an unhealthy preference for booze. With minimal skills, and little formal education, each man searched for his identity, and some success at something.

Ike remembered the speed with which the organization had come together. Performers, trainers and their animals, midgets, musicians, and laborers converged from their winter hibernation. Advance people had already been on the road ahead of the schedule arranging advertising, and checking on details with the town governments, checking the proposed circus grounds, clearing details with their sponsors in each town and village. Ike thought it must be much like this in an ant hill. Once the organization started rolling, it was like perpetual motion. Only catastrophe could stop the machine. Each day was the same, yet different. Someone would be sick, or get hurt. An animal would get loose and have to be rounded up. And Betsie needed to be watched and tended most of the time.

All the elephants were called bulls, but all were actually cows.

Bulls were too temperamental and unmanageable when a cow came into heat. Ike was quick to learn the commands needed to encourage Betsie in her work. Besides being a center-ring performer, she was important in the process of raising the large tents.

Ike remembered being amazed at the tent-raising process he had witnessed at Hayes, Kansas, so many years ago but now he was in the middle of it. The advance crew from the advance train would haul out the canvas, position it over its proposed location, and set the side poles, which raised the outside edge of the big top. Center poles would be set. The center poles were rigged with ropes and pulleys, and were attached to the tent by use of a large ring called a "Bale Ring". Betsie would be hitched to the rope; and by pulling slowly and carefully, the center section of the tent would be lifted from the ground to the top of the pole. As the raising advanced, other crew members placed the quarter poles, and the roustabouts would begin placing the stakes. Eight men with sledge hammers would circle the stake. Each in precise turn would strike until the crew boss would yell "Hold". Another crew following after them would skillfully loop the guy rope over the stake. Six to eight husky forms would grasp the line above the stake and pull it taut five or six times to "Guy Out" the big tents. The stake man would secure the line and they would move on to the next. Repetition had joined perfection with a smooth, systematic functioning team.

It was amazing—the precision and hard work it took to move, set up, show, feed, clothe, perform, break down, load the forty-car train, move, and start the whole thing over again. Usually the show lasted only one day. He was lucky for his first show where

IKE: A FIREFLY LIFE

they were in one spot, in Chicago, for fifteen days then in St. Louis for four more.

Ike was paid seven dollars and fifty cents per week, and slept on a lousy, vermin infested cot, when he could sleep. Usually he had at least two meals a day, but on some days the cook would prepare "dookey" bags with maybe an apple and a peanut butter sandwich to eat when he could during the day. He didn't get a chance to see the performance of the shows, as he was with the elephants. He was constantly watching them, or preparing them for their acts in the "big top". Each cow had to be washed down, and their gear (costumes) put on before their act, and changed between entrances. They had to be led to the nearest water source each day, and the ground had to be cleaned up after them as much as possible.

He was not stepped on by any of the cows. In fact, he was constantly impressed by the calm deliberate step and the gentle nature displayed by each one. The truth was that some times, one would get spooked and go on a rampage, so he had to always be aware of the animals moods. Usually, with proper feed and water, together with firm gentle treatment, the scene around the elephants was quiet. There was always something to be done from the time the train was unloaded until Betsie was back on board.

He found many kindred spirits working with him on the crew—men without work, or running from something—the law or their family. From the managers, performers, and on through all the working groups, it was a cohesive, smoothly functioning body. He felt he belonged, which warmed his spirit. He felt an acceptance and understanding from non-judgmental fellow travelers. There was no past, and not much future beyond

79

tomorrow. But eventually the feeling of being on a treadmill, working like hell and not getting anyplace, became a strong realization. He knew this could go on only so long. He felt he could possibly return to Peru and work with the menagerie through the winter, but eventually even that lost appeal. He had been with the show through its fifteen days in Chicago, then four days in St. Louis, East St. Louis, Vincennes, Evansville, then Louisville.

The guilt of abandoning the family back in Bartonia, Indiana, weighed on him. Someone was needed to help harvest the fall crops. So, after this month of travel throughout the Midwest, he wrote a letter saying, "Come meet me in Louisville. I'm ready to come home."

The strained and embarrassing meeting in the dawn's light at the Louisville train yard, washed over him and filled him anew with the futility of his adventure, his attempt to escape from the meaninglessness of his existence, and from depression, fear, and helplessness. He was now aware he would carry the emptiness to his grave. That was all there was for him. Overriding the merry times which spotted his life, was the pall of failure to hold his life together, or to accomplish anything, to come to the end alone with no one to say, "You gave it a good try, Ike." Some have said it is not the goal, but the journey that is important. Well, I've had one crazy journey.

* * * *

He lifted the package of ready-made Camel cigarettes from his bedside table. *Ain't technology great? Seems like I've spent much of my life rolling my cigarettes. I kinda miss the challenge of getting a well-filled properly shaped weed on my own. These youngsters missed the great challenge. I'll have to show these guys how we did it in the old days. Doc said I should stop smoking, but I can't see it will do any harm now. I can't breath when I'm not smoking either.*

He rolled his chair over to the table at the end of the ward, looked through the day's papers which had been brought in by the orderly. It was just a re-hash of the news heard on the radio and offered no interest to him. His thoughts would not stay focused. He faded in and out of awareness. A fuzzy feeling, not being connected, not caring, not aware, and then lucidity again. Was he just tired? Nothing mattered to him. It must be the fever working at the edge of his consciousness.

The rest of the day passed in confusion. He sensed a flurry of mental pictures of past days, but none fitted into a pattern of thought; there was family, past jobs, days in the hospital, rented houses that were quickly abandoned, his wife's pain and nagging, lost days of wandering in confusion, seeking purpose.

Supper was left untouched, for his bed beckoned to him early. With the nurse's help, he fell heavily onto the firm mattress, and was soon asleep.

July 6, 1962

Ike awoke at the break of dawn. The orange sun cast long bands of light across the floor and up the west wall. Already, one could feel the promise of oppressive heat and humidity for this day. He was aware of his inner heat as well and found it hard to collect his thoughts. His mind kept wandering, unable to focus on anything for long. He knew his fever was still with him. He rang for the nurse. Within five minutes, the nurse strolled into the ward, and pushed the "shut off" button on the wall by the bed.

"What's up soldier?"

"Better take my temp again. I am burning up."

"You do look a little flushed this morning, and I don't think it's the light. Be back in a sec. Okay?"

An unexpected calm moved through his body. He had a sense of letting go, relaxing, and accepting his situation. His flashes of long-ago memories, the past years, which caused so many regrets now sloughed off, and he felt less the pangs of those unanswered wishes. Now, it was too late to change himself and certainly the past. Maybe, it was the effects of his fever. Maybe it was his general weakness. Maybe a recognition of the coming end of all pain. He lay in bed awaiting the return of the nurse.

He slept fitfully. Dreamed. He was dancing in a square dance. The fiddles, banjoes, and guitars were whacking out "Turkey in the Straw". He was swinging Emma in a "Meet Your Partner", followed by a "Do-si-do", then open fields of flowing grain, endless horizons, gusts of wind-driven dust, white fluffy clouds, swirling and growing overhead, running from...from what? He could not see. Running...short of breath...gasping...running from the unseen...then a calm again...a small white house in the middle of fields of corn...then bars... He was caged, surrounded with filth and unshaven bums, vomit and urine smells...vision of fluffy clouds...a mountain valley...a warm sparkling stream...on the bank, fishing pole in hand, skipping rocks across the water...mother and father standing on the porch...a gray colored cabin....

"Ike? Here's your aspirin." The nurse placed his hand under Ike's head, elevated him to reach the straw.

"Looks like we're gonna have a scorcher today. That ain't gonna help ya much, Ike."

"Don't matter. I'll just have to take what I get. Ain't that the way it is?"

Other vets began to waken and grasp what they could of the day. Another day of sameness begins again.

Ike thought, maybe he could get out on the verandah today, if he could hustle up the strength.

The nurse was quietly helping each vet as needed, providing

urinals, holding wheel chairs, lifting into wheel chairs, adjusting straps, combing hair, shaving those without arms, carrying on a quiet banter with one and all.

Across the way, Larry said, "Gonna be hotter than a napalm fart. When ya gonna get more fans in this steamin' mad house?" Larry had been caught in an ambush. Both arms had been amputated after extreme damage from machine gun fire. He was in for fitting a new prosthesis. He expected to be released as soon as the physical therapist was satisfied that he was at ease with the new devices, which would transform his life to "normal" again. So, Larry, was in a rare spirit today anticipating getting out and heading back to his lovely family. Everyone on the ward had seen pictures of his wife and kids at least twice in the last two weeks.

For many, the pictures were a bitter-sweet experience. Some missed the family they could never have; others thought of families lost, or traumatized by their neurotic behavior—or unable to provide a supporting relationship with one so miserably maimed in body and mind.

But for Larry, his patient wife had given him love, family, and courage to move ahead with his life; and now he could see possibilities for new and better job opportunities. He had cause for his joyful hope.

Those most maimed never talked about their misery but grasped the fear and pain with a white-knuckled passion of dread. The agony and fear was held in deepest private caverns of their being while eating at their vitality. It was often covered up with crude macho flippant bravado, which they used as their prosthesis for getting through life.

Ike could see this in some of the boys as he had given in to some of the same patterns recently, but not now. Finally he had to let go of the anger and despair. His persona was now that of a quiet, but not cheerful, acceptance of his fate if that is what it must be considered... *"No! Not fate. This is just the way it is. Everyone has some suffering, some joy, some successes, and some failures. Just because a person gets caught up in history of which he is a part but yet not of his making, (as far as one can tell) does not qualify as fate. But there was still room for doubt. What difference does it make anyway? You took what was dealt. Sometimes it is clear how the hand is to be played, but most of the time it is just do the best you can. Is that fate? Oh, well, my hand is about played out I feel...and that's okay. After seventy-two years, you can't expect to have many cards left. Too many wasted tricks."*....

* * * *

It's not surprising that Ike kept returning to farm labor as that was the work he knew best. It was also the work that fulfilled his need for space and freedom. The work of a factory was more confinement and dirt than he could take.

Before the war, he had worked as a molder in the International Harvester Foundry. If ever there was a hard, dirty, dangerous job, that was one; and one to which he never thought to return. His brother, Bob, had worked for years as a core-man in the foundry. That job was less heavy and dangerous, but a dirty mess none the less. It too was not a job he would seek. Soon after mustering out of the service, he found a job as a trimmer at a factory which made seats for the car manufacturer in Richmond. He had become quite proficient at that job. His major tool was a hammer, one head of which was magnetized. He would position an upholstering tack (head first between his lips) from a reservoir of twenty or thirty held in his mouth. He would extract the tack with the magnetic head, drive the tack into the upholster cloth and the wood frame, flip the hammer over and drive the tack with the non-magnetic side of the head. The process was accomplished with rapid dexterity. No recorded incident of swallowing tacks was ever reported.

He lost his job and his partially completed house during the crash of '29. He was grateful for Roosevelt's creation of the WPA, through which he was able to keep food on the table. Much of the work done with WPA was paved-road construction and other right-of-way improvement. When that program had offered all it could, he was back to working as a farm hand again.

One farm family brought Ike onto its spread several times (three to be exact). It was the Zachariah Stanley farm, situated on the C&O Railroad line about three miles south of Boston, Indiana. This was the same area into which his parents had moved when arriving from Virginia.

Zach was a small wiry man, whose age and health dictated the need for manual labor assistance. His wife, Elizabeth, was an imposing, stately, educated woman. Ironically for Ike, she was the national president for the Women's Christian Temperance Union. There was no doubt in Ike's mind as to who ran the Stanley farmstead.

Zach had eighty acres of gently-rolling farm land complete with creek fed, sheltering wood land. A small white clap-board bungalow was situated on the South side of the gravel road that cut through the acreage. The house had five rooms on the main floor and a loft, large enough to accommodate another bedroom.

There was a large yard, garden, chicken house, wood shed, and a two-story barn/corn crib on the property. The garden kept the household in food. Ike's meager pay and the monthly disability check kept the family clothed. Emma canned vegetables, fruit, meat, sauerkraut, and stored them in the cellar. She generally kept the household in order. It was a nice location with easy access to Richmond, which was about eight miles north on Highway 27.

All the farming was horse-powered, but Ike did not mind that at all. And, despite his problem with alcohol, he and Elizabeth Stanley kept a civil relationship, though admittedly she was quick to preach the sin and depravation of the awful drug. Little did she suspect that Ike was making "home brew" in the little house across the road.

Zach and Elizabeth had two sons, Earl and Jay. Earl was a Chevrolet salesman in California; Jay was an attorney in Richmond. Upon Zach's death in '35 Earl, with wife and child, returned to the farm to take over.

Elizabeth couldn't handle it on her own, and neither could her son, Earl. He was not cut out to do farming, but at the urging of Jay, came home to help his mother as much as possible. He was physically soft having lifted nothing more than a sales brochure, so to speak. He and she needed help to keep the farm viable. It was difficult to succeed with only seventy tillable acres.

Earl's wife soon tired of the confinement of farm living, She left, in less than a year, returning to California for good. Ike, however, made the difference; and along with Emma and son Bobby, and Earl's son, Earl Jr., there were enough hands to handle the operation.

Between 1937 and 1939 Ike had moved in and out of the

Stanley tenant cottage twice. The third time he moved back to help on the Stanley farm was after Elizabeth's death. In 1940, Earl suggested Ike move into the big residence and live with him as family. This arrangement lasted for about a year and then Ike found he could no longer work with Earl.

The daily activities went smoothly enough. There was no argument or major noticeable problem. Deep within though, Ike resented Earl Stanley. Earl was a college-educated man. Without meaning to, he had made Ike feel inferior in many ways. Ike was smarter about farming than Earl could ever be, and in that regard, found Earl's book-learning not worth much. He could see Earl was out of his element—soft, partially crippled in his left elbow from a car accident suffered in California—and really not able to carry his share of the heavy work load. Emma and Bobby seemed content (too content actually), and Ike was jealous because of the obvious high regard both, Emma and Bobby, held for Earl. Ike was just uncomfortable and had stayed long enough. The wanderlust had struck again. He had to get out of this situation. He wanted to move back to town.

Though he argued at length with Emma, she would not move again. She said, "Ike, you have moved us thirteen places in the last eight years, and I am not going to move Bobby again. He is happy in school here, doing well, has lots of friends, and I will not uproot him again. You go wherever and whenever you have to, but I am staying here if Earl does not object."

This only confirmed his conviction of Emma's love for Earl. He left his family on the farm, and moved to Richmond. That too was without succes—No family, no decent place to live, only occasional earnings from sundry jobs. He never regretted moving away from the farm and didn't really miss his family that much. He was sick and tired of Emma's constant nagging and know-it-all attitude. She did hold his life together somewhat, but even in the best of times he was not comfortable,.

He thought of getting a divorce but decided not to. It was better for Emma to continue receiving his veteran's disability check to help her and Bobby survive. He would make it on his own. World War II was going full blast. Work was plentiful as long as he remained sober....

* * * *

Why had he dropped into this recall of his family again today? It was surely his loneliness, which he had to admit had been with him for many days now. He needed to be doing something. He could still tell his fever was elevated. He was feeling the fatigue, which goes with fever.

The nurse brought the breakfast cart and his pills. "I'll work on your cough again this morning, Ike, just as soon as I get this breakfast passed around. You sound filled with phlegm as usual."

"Don't guess that is likely to change much."

"Nope, I guess not, but maybe we can give you some relief."

True to his work, the nurse helped Ike roll onto his side, and preceded to thump his back with the heel of his hand. After a few minutes of this therapy, the phlegm began to loosen up and Ike was able to get rid of some of it, but his cough, though more productive, was nonem the less persistent. He was totally fatigued after each coughing spasm, and he would lay back on his pillow gasping for air until the next spasm over took his whole body. By mid-morning he was able to get out of bed with the nurse's help. The nurse pulled back the covers, placed his arms under Ike's diminished body, and gently sat him in the padded seat. With a few minor adjustments of the posterior, reasonable comfort was attained. Another day to test his endurance had begun.

He had gained no strength, and felt the need for support in order to keep him from sliding out of the wheel chair. He turned the radio on to catch the daily morning news....

[European sector of Oran, Algeria is in a panic, as more fighting rages following independence from France...over 210 killed in yesterday's fighting] *Now that's no news. They are going to keep that up until there will be no one left to enjoy their new freedom from the French....*[The first "H bomb" was exploded underground in Nevada. Authorities announce plans to detonate another one tomorrow above ground...military officials suggest atomic explosions might, in the future, be economically used to build new harbor and canals]... *A bombs / H bombs? What does it mean? How can we get all that power out of a tiny atom? What the hell is an atom anyway? What will they play with next?....*

[A battle is raging near Saigon....] *Saigon? Where is Saigon? What are we doing there? Are those people communist too? Who are the good guys? Is there any way to tell the difference?* [A trade alliance with Europe is being debated in the House...Kennedy is considering tax cuts, but is watching economic trends...weather...fair and calm...] *And hot too. Don't need a weather station to predict that fact....*

Atomic bombs, hydrogen bombs, My God! what is in store for us? I have lived through the most amazing time...all the new things developed by the scientists and technicians is beyond anything I could have imagined as a child. I was a young man when I saw the first automobile. I thought that was about the most amazing contraption. My first car was a model T Ford. I remember Emma, trying to learn to drive it, pushed the reverse pedal and almost backed over me. I was in the army before I saw the real development of planes. I knew the Wright brothers had developed the airplane, but I realized how important they had become as we saw them in action over France. And now, we are ready to put something in orbit around the world. How, in the name of God, is that possible. It just seems there is nothing we can't develop now. And the increased use of television, now that and the radio are truly beyond my mind. How is it possible to communicate by just sending message over the air? And now, to show pictures the same way...I just don't know? I think of all the things electricity has brought to the families; besides the radio. The electric cook stove and refrigeration have been so important, and modern inside plumbing sure beats the outside "one holers". It has been a great time of change, these last seventy-two years. Our fine, young, crazy president wants to put men on the moon. We can't do that...and if we could, why would we want to? I wonder what the future holds? I would like to stay around and see what is coming next.

He felt the need for fresh air. The ward was becoming oppressive. He was imprisoned in his ward and in his wheel chair. He needed to get outside, even if he was terribly weak.

"Sure would like to get out on the verandah for awhile. Do you think I could get out there pretty soon?" he asked the nurse.

"I will call an aide to take you out right now if you like."

"Yeah, that would be fine; let's do it when you can. Okay?"

"We can do that. I'll ask the aide to come in pretty soon. Then we will get you out of here."

As he sat quietly looking out the window, and began to feel a strange tingling in his right arm and right side of his face. He could not lift his right arm, and his head felt strangely disconnected from his body. He had never had any feeling similar to this before. He said to his bed neighbor, "I don't know what's goin' on, but I'm havin' a very strange feelin'."

"Think we ought to get the nurse back in here?"

Ike flexed his body a little, moved his head around to test his muscles, and noted if anything else was feeling strange. He said, "Don't reckon its much of anythin'. Just the effects of this fever I guess."

The tingling feeling and the disorientation slowly passed, and soon he felt the same as before. He couldn't imagine any cause but the fever for this strange feeling and passed it off as just one of those crazy things. He did not mention it to the nurse, since it had passed so quickly.

Some soulful country music was being played on the radio. Ike sat with his eyes closed and listened to balladeers whine away their blues of lost loves and "he-done-me-wrongs".

A rosy-faced orderly bounced into the room promptly at 10:00, and Ike was ceremoniously rolled to the big double doors at the end of the hall. The wheel chair was turned one hundred eighty degrees and the orderly pushed the panic bar with her substantial butt, opened the door and pulled Ike, in reverse, over the metal threshold.

He was actually refreshed by the hot air that greeted his exit, while the sun gave a lift akin to new freedom. The warm, humid air felt good to his wasted lungs. He was placed so the sun was on his back. He was able to look across the substantial grounds; his eyes followed the course of several driveways. Lined by tree tops, their green boughs contrasted beautifully against the cloudless blue of this summer morning sky.

The confinement in the ward became almost unbearable for

Ike after only a few days. It was important for him to get into the fresh air as much as possible. The sun never did work hardship on him, for he had survived the worst it could send. His sun-reddened skin on face and neck abruptly ended at the collar line; and although somewhat paled from its former deep copper-red tone, it would clearly mark him as one having spent many years working under this furnace of life.

He realized he felt good about the work he had done over the years. He had worked hard always giving an honest day's work. If only he could have overcome his desire to spend his earned money on a liquid diet, he might have felt even better about himself.

Next to the heat of summer, he liked the fall weather best. It occurred to him he may be connecting that feeling with the satisfaction of reaping the harvest of the spring and summer crops. Only the corn remained in the field to be gathered before the first snow if possible. Often corn shucking would not be over by then. Although it was hard work, it was a good feeling to walk through the rows of ripened corn, ripping the golden ears from their neat cover, and quickly tossing them into the wagon. Thousands of times this action would be repeated. The shucked ears bouncing off the backboard and into the wagon time after time developed a rhythm. The wagon sideboard on the opposite side contained more boards, and was three feet higher by than the near sideboard. One did not have to look where he was throwing, as he would never be likely to throw hard enough to clear the raised side.

On one occasion though, Ike did recall an ear of corn slipping as it was tossed, (missing the wagon completely), and striking

Maude, the old "gee" mare, on the rump. A startled lunge foreword on a downhill slope gave way to a trot, and the team went racing across the field. They gave no heed to Ike and the kids running along behind shouting "whoa! Whoa. WHOA!" At the end of the field, the team turned left, caught the corner of the wagon in the wire fence and ripped out about sixteen feet. By then, one of the kids had run to the head of the team, grabbed one rein, and got them to yield their interest in pulling out more fence line. It seemed something was always ready to go wrong to make the day interesting, and to give more work.

The cool crisp air of the fall, the smell of burning leaves, the rich color of the trees, made it seem too beautiful to believe. Each year, he felt this same rich appreciation of the season. He thought on it again as he sat under the hot July sun.

The airing lasted until 11:45, when everyone interested had to be back on the ward for lunch. Though he had little desire for food at this time, he consented to return to the ward with the rest of the sun-lovers. Nothing of the proffered bland food appealed to him. He drank some tepid coffee, ate a slice of buttered bread, and sipped a couple spoons full of noodle soup which was as bland as tap water. Good thing I'm not hungry, he thought.

It was still hot in the ward, but it seemed cool by contrast to the verandah's deck which reflected the sun like an oven. He was glad to have been outside none the less. It was a chance to know he was a part of something other than the hospital ward.

This was the hardest of any of the several visits to the hospital Ike had made over the years. Other visits had usually come after an unusually bad drunk, when his general health was dissipated, and he could not function alone. The stays provided a time for him to get 'dried out', and gain some weight, and get a new perspective on what he was doing with his life. This visit, however, was depressing in that it was a dramatic, abrupt turn around, and brought him to the point of a final if not reluctant acceptance of his own complicity in his down-fall.

Time passed quickly during the afternoon with little activity. Time had a way of roaring by unnoticed. As he got older, there was less and less time available each day. He was sure the day must be at least two hours shorter than when he was a youth when he enjoyed great blocks of time. At that time he couldn't wait to be older, get a job, go to war, have a family; and time moved so slowly then. Now, there was no accounting for the swiftness of time's bounding ahead, pulling him unwillingly, faster and faster into its oblivion. Maybe time is nothing more than man's awareness of himself, awareness of cycles, seasons, and events which happened in linear progression like falling dominoes. In any case, he was aware of being in a tidal wave of time in which he was helpless to do anything but wait until finally he was cast down into the endless abyss. If you can't beat it, don't fret about it. That was where he always ended up in his thinking.

The newspaper articles just echoed the morning radio news. The only things worth reading were the cartoons anyway. This afternoon the cartoons were blurry, his eyes were not well served anymore by the store-bought reading glasses. He began to feel the strange tingling numbness down his right arm again. It was the same feeling he had experienced earlier. It made him feel weaker, slightly dizzy, and it put a final smashing end to the small amount of energy allotted to him today. He had to get back in bed for he had reached the end of his day. It was only four thirty PM.

When evening meal came, he drank a glass of milk and ate a couple bites of green beans and meat loaf. There was no taste to any of the food. He lay back on his pillow and stared at the ceiling until he was soon asleep, unaware as the food tray was removed and his bed cranked down for the night.

July 7, 1962

Slowly, the horrors of nightmares, the helpless unwanted memories, the night sweats, gave way to the blessed relief of another dawning. Gradually, the reality of a new day singularly stirred the conscious network of his mind. Each of the veterans, in his own tortured time, bed by bed, willingly opened his eyes with relief, thankful for the security of bed and care for another day. It was not the lap of luxury, but it was much better than many alternatives. Yawning, throat clearing, stretching limbs, for those with limbs to stretch, slow, agonizing exits from bed followed by trips to the "head" for those few who were ambulatory. The faint sounds of activity, evidence of life on the ward, stirred the ambient air with its faint charge.

Not so with Ike. On this morning, he was oblivious. A faint snoring issued from his pillow. He was on his right side, right hand flat under his right cheek, left hand tucked between his legs, his thighs were drawn up in a semi-fetal position. This was his chosen sleeping position. On this morning, he was in his own personal world, unaffected by the morning declaration of existing life.

His snoring stopped. His sleep continued until everyone on the ward had been up for some time. His mind slowly shifted from its dream mode. He was not sure whether he was awake or not. Faintly aware of sound, eyes not yet open, he remained in the uncertain middle world between dream and reality. It was inviting to stay in the middle world. Consciousness was a pain for body and spirit. Why not just stay in this inanimate realm as long as possible?

He lay quietly listening to the familiar ward sounds, vaguely aware of the nurse standing by his bed, but acknowledged nothing by opening his eyes. He was content to relax and let it all pass.

Is this another day he wants to face? It was inevitable. You can't just ignore it. Sooner or later you have to move into the stream of the living day. Since that was that, he slowly opened his eyes and discovered a day just like yesterday. The sun was higher than usual at his awakening. He wondered how late he had slept. Breakfast trays were standing in their cart at the door. Were they on the way in or out? It was just time for breakfast, and he was not ready for either, the breakfast or the day.

His right hand was asleep from lack of circulation, but he managed to reach the bed regulator buttons, and lift the head of his bed. The nurse approached the bed when he heard the motor. He automatically handed Ike the urinal bottle.

"I think I will need two of these, the way my bladder feels this mornin'. I'm about to wash away."

"Ike, you're just shriveled up. Even all that beer hasn't

stretched your bladder none." The nurse smiled as he walked out to get the breakfast trays.

Ike just looked at his breakfast as it was placed on the bed tray. The usual fare presented there was uninviting hot (tepid) coffee, toast, a poached egg and a round slice of fried black sausage. Not too bad a selection if prepared right; and if he felt like eating it, but he didn't and it wasn't.

The nurse retrieved the urinal. "You going to eat any of this great breakfast? You surely do need to eat more. You ain't eatin' enough Ike. You gotta have somethin in your system to help fight that pneumonia."

"Yeah, I know. I may drink some coffee after I get shaved. It won't be much colder then than it is now. You have time to shave me?"

"Yep, just as soon as I get all the hogs slopped. I'll be back soon. Why don't you try some toast and coffee while I finish. It won't hurt ya none."

Ike reached for the toast and slowly took a bite. It was buttered, but barely. He reached for the coffee mug and found it was difficult for him to lift.

What the hell? I am so weak, the coffee mug seems heavy. Better take it slow and careful. I still have a fever. I'm sure of it.

He managed to drink about half his coffee. Even with cream and sugar, the coffee tasted like it had been brewed over the open fire and boiled for an hour. He had two bites of over-fried sausage.

I used to make better sausage than that, when Andy and I butchered hogs back in the 30's. One day we killed and processed three two hundred pound barrows. We made some great sausage from those big guys along with several

101

cakes of *cracklins. The women ground much of the meat, seasoned it; and stuffed it into links. Some of it was canned. But that sausage was better than any I've tasted since.*

The nurse returned, and said, "Well, I see you ate somethin', but it ain't enough to give you any help."

"It tasted like it looks. Besides, I ain't even able to hold the damn coffee mug. Now, ain't that a good one?"

The nurse lifted him onto his right side and proceeded to thump him on the back as before. The routine produced the usual, expected round of coughing and dislodging of accumulated phlegm. The breathing was only slightly improved by the procedure. Ike lay back trying to take deep breaths. The breathing was more like gasping as he fought to get enough air. He felt light-headed, weak and disoriented much of the time. This was not unusual for him during the morning effort to clear his lungs, but now it took longer than it did a few days ago. He was surely much weaker.

"Let me just lay here awhile and then see if I feel like getting into my favorite racing chair a little later." Ike smiled and winked at the nurse, who smiled back and went on to other patients.

A radio, near by, was broadcasting the morning news. Ike lay with his eyes closed and his mind tuned in....

[In a statement to the press, yesterday, Robert McNamara expressed optimism about the tide of military developments, stating the tide was turning against the communist guerrilla forces...the ratio of killed and captured was now favorable to the south]....*Well, that's good news. Maybe we can get our lads back home. Don't know what we're doin over there anyway. Those people can take care of themselves. Can't say I know why we are there, but we gotta stop those commies I guess...*[William Faulkner was found dead in his home yesterday of an apparent heart attack. Mr. Faulkner became renowned for his many novels about the Deep South. He was sixty-four years old...] [A grim disclosure today, reports on the people in East Berlin trying to escape the oppressive communist government. On June 26th a battle developed in a newly-dug escape tunnel. One was killed and at least three wounded. There is no record of the identity of the victims... No one knows how many East Berlin citizens have successfully escaped into West Berlin, or how many may have been killed or wounded in the attempt...] *never heard much about communism until after WWII...can't say I was ever told much about it. Everyone seems to think it will take over the world...It must be bad if people are risking their lives to get away from it... It's all kinda mixed up in this old world....*

The news droned on. Sports news in brief...Ike caught the important part...[Cincinnati lost to Houston Colts yesterday. Pitcher Joey Jay was the winning pitcher, assisted by two runs in the second inning, which was the final two to nothing. Reds now stand fifth (still) in the league with forty three wins and thirty six losses...] [In the entertainment field, Bob Hope and Bing Crosby are on the road again. The film, "Road to Hong Kong," is now showing and drawing big audiences....]

The news was always different and always the same, but each day they were bound to hear it. It was "the way" to keeps in touch with the outside world. Though not in prison, the men on the ward felt isolated from life and family. It was important to keep in touch even if the news was repetitive.

"Hey, Ike! Get your lazy ass outa bed. It's almost noon. You glued to the sheet today? We gotta get in a game of euchre sometime today. Just kiddin', man. But, you'll feel better if you get up and move around a bit. Come on get your old skinny ass a movin'."

Ike smiled and said. "That's easy for you to say. Ya young hot head. Wait till your old machine has as many miles on it as mine. Christ! The way you are burning up the road, you won't make it to seventy two years. So, don't give me all that rah rah crap. I'll get up when I damn well want to, and I can beat you at euchre any time, unless of course we are partners. Now that sounds like a winner. Hot Wheels and Wheeze Bag take on all comers. Well, if I decide to get out of the comfy bed, you've got yourself a player. We'll see. We Will See."

Maybe I oughta get up. Just too weak...maybe it will give me a little strength if I sit up awhile... Need to move about some to help these old lungs...or so the doctor says...I don't wonna get up....

What seemed like a half hour of commercials passed, some good ol' country music was now playing, Some sick sounding female has been done wrong again. The music played on. Some of it was foot-tappin' good, but he wasn't even able to wiggle his toes in time with the music. *Sure would love to go square dancin agin'....*

He rang for the nurse, reluctantly deciding it was best to get up. Maybe he would feel better. He surely couldn't feel any weaker.

"Hey, Ike, I said I would shave ya. Want to do that now before I lift you out?"

"Yeah, I guess so. Don't make much difference, Ain't gonna have any visitors anyway."

"Well, it might freshen ya up a little."

The shaving was interrupted several times by the continued

coughing; but eventually, shaven and lifted into his wheelchair, Ike was forced to face the day, and survive the coughing spasms that never seemed to let up. He managed to get some air into his lungs by gasping several times a minute. He was plagued by continual light-headed feelings, adding to his fatigue and general disorientation.

I can't make it today. I can't...even roll this damn chair...what am I gonna do?...Jesus, I hate to be so helpless... How? Why? I've lived too damn long... What do I have to show for it?... Not a hellava lot!...These years have gone so fast...let me try them again...Yes! Maybe, maybe I could get somethin right next time around...I never thought I would be rich, but I would be happier if I could do it over again...But, I'm back again, right where I was yesterday...I've got what I got and that is all there is to it...I can't go back and change a damn thing...But, I don't have to like it.

"Come on Ike. Don't just sit there. I'm bored silly with this damn do-nothin life. Let's play. Let's PLAY! Yeah!"

Slowly pushing the wheels of his chair, Ike inched over to the table at the end of the ward. He and Hot Wheels decided to take on all comers. Hot Wheels dealt, turned up the jack of clubs.

"Pass"

Ike said, "take 'er up. That's the best I got." He was sitting with the jack of spades, ace and king of clubs, and ace and king of spades. He trumped a heart lead. Then led from his clubs, and quickly took all the tricks.

"Hot damn! Four points for Wheeze Bag and Hot Wheels. You guys give up?" Ike was doing his best to keep his spirits and his energy up long enough to finish the next few hands.

The game moved on—a point here and a point there, until Ike finally won ten to nine. Even with the "no brains" hand at the start, it was all he could do to keep his mind on the game, and was lucky to come out a winner.

"I'm sorry partner. It was a good game, thanks to you, but I ain't up to playin' any more. Takes too much concentration. I ain't able to keep my mind on the game. Come on in here 'smart ass', take my place. I'll watch for awhile." he said to an active kibitzer.

Hot Wheels understood what Ike was saying, but had no way of knowing how weak he was feeling. It could be seen, however, in the lines of Ike's face and the posture of his wasted body.

The oxygen was not circulating today. All attempts to stay alert failed to keep his body and mind at a constant level of awareness. He would come into a conscious state only to be aware of coming out of an unconscious one. Dizziness, an occasional strange dead feeling along his right side, and extreme heaviness in his chest, came in surges like waves along the shore and seemed to wear him away. His occasional gasp for added oxygen had no apparent positive effect.

He managed to stay upright in his chair. He found himself aimlessly staring out the window, only mildly aware of the activities in the ward. The swells of emotion he once felt were now eddies of confused acceptance. There was no fight (no ups and downs) only the stoic acceptance of the situation as it was. He would have, at another time in his life, yelled and cursed the world in general for his helplessness.

He felt another helplessness during the depression years. There too, he was a victim. He struggled then. He was mad at the world, at the government, at the lack of jobs, at himself. He took solace in being one of the millions of Americans without work, who stood in a commissary line, waiting for a handout of bread, potatoes, cheese, or whatever the government had on hand to help out the unemployed and hungry families. He spent days upon days looking for work. He fought the best he could. The work for a time with WPA helped to get the family through. He had fought and lost. He had been angry and lost. It was like his situation now. He was not in control of his circumstances. But now he cared less, and had no inclination for change.

Supper trays were rolled onto the ward. Ike ate at the table. It was easier to do that than to get back in bed and get adjusted to eat from the tray. He did not feel like eating anything. The coffee was hot this time. The Swiss steak was well-drowned in brown gravy. The gravy was tasty. The steak was tough. The Jello was also tough and rubbery. *How in this world can they ruin Jello?* He ate very little, and pushed away from the table. He usually sat around and shot the bull with the guys, but not this evening. He needed to get to bed and ease his body's tension.

He needed the nurse quickly, else he just might fall out on his head. He called out to get some attention. He was quickly satisfied with getting out of his chair, but was less satisfied with the lack of comfort found in bed. His breathing was decidedly more difficult. He just could not get enough air. As each gasp seemed less effective than the last, it produced a feeling of panic. It would be difficult to stay focused.

He felt a relaxed calm. There was a sense of joy, or maybe peace. Ike felt as if all his life came together. He felt the excitement holding his new infant sons, and remembered the amazement of watching them grow. He warmed in the realization that he too had been loved and nurtured. He felt the warmth of Emmas cheek, and her fun-loving personality. He heard the old country songs sung with his brothers, and the comradery of his drinking buddies. Through it all, he had had hope, and always good intentions. There was a sense of peace about it, for he had fought the good fight and that was all he could do. There was a warm glow.

July 8, 1962

The fire flies signaled in the darkened meadow. Each, having clung to its grassy stem by day, now rose into the black of night. Like earth bound stars, unable to sustain light as if short-circuited, they signal, "Here Am I. Choose Me". Over and over, they signal their cold fire of affirmation. This, seemingly peaceful scene is, in fact, a surging mass of living energy, searching for connection, for recognition, for a partner.

* * * *

Ice cold, spring water, flows quietly into the mountain brook, a trickle, gathers together with brother springs, falls, races. rolls toward their destiny. Together, amassed, their individuality is lost to the one great surge of falling, pulsing, ebbing, rushing, power; the power pooled and deferred by a great dam. Kinetic energy is sitting, waiting to surge on to generate power or evaporate into the valley mist.

Gold and red, robbed of its chlorophyll, the mountain oak leaf, having given all its services to the mighty oak, awaits the calling of the passing breeze to gently set it on the ground. There, to begin the cycle again, losing itself into basic elements of transformed earth. Now to feed the roots, where before it had transformed the sky, the energy force changed, to be part of the whole, it lives on, the cycle is completed.

From Ike's primal center, there pulsed an ancient knowledge of the cycle of all things. He could not be, nor did he care to be, set aside as different from the naturer's flow. It is beautiful simplicity. Out of the seeming chaos, Ike knew the ultimate simplicity of returning to basic form, and rebuilding complicated structures.

Is it by chance? Is it by design? Is there a guiding force? Does it have a plan? Is it playing dice with the chaos of the stars? I am surely a part of the system, but I seem so insignificant. Yet, all other things in nature, taken singularly are insignificant, taken as a whole, all are necessary. And so am I.

With these visions from the early morning pre-awakening, Ike stirred with a calm awareness, as he opened his eyes on the new day. It was a glorious sunny morning. He welcomed it without dread, as had been his custom during so many weeks of confinement.

There would be continued warmth today. The sun was beaming its morning spotlight on the floor and wall. The men were returning to their insignificant roles in the chaos.

How clearly he felt the power of his vision. Somewhere during the night he had seen all of his past life as nothing asd as every everything; he was a part of the great chaos. The chaos did not matter, but that he was a part of it did matter. He became calm inside.

The ritual of his morning coughing continued, but was helped not at all by the nurses thumping on his back. His gasping for air barely aided his intake of oxygen. His weakness was paramount. He thought of the oak leaf.

Breakfast coffee helped clear his throat. The dry toast was uninviting as was the cold egg. He didn't think he needed to eat this morning.

Once, comfortably placed in his chair, he asked to be rolled over to the beam of sunlight still bathing the floor. There, with eyes partially closed, he drank in the warmth of its power. His eyes closed. He opened them, and the sun no longer warmed him. It was too high to shine its warmth on his withered body, and he wondered how long he had been sitting there. His body was cold now. It missed the warmth of the life-giving sun.

He felt the tingling sensation on his right side again. His vision blurred and then cleared, and blurred again. It was the strange feeling he had experienced over the past few days, from time to time. Maybe he was not getting enough oxygen to keep the machinery running. Maybe, maybe.

He looked down at the stumps of his legs. *Seems we've been about as far as we can go on this trip. It was one hell of a trip. Old legs I really missed ya. You did all you could. What a damned way to live!*

The strange feeling of numbness gushed across his upper torso. He noticed, his toes had stopped itching. He tried to lift his hand to scratch his nose. It would not move. He heard Hot Wheels say. "Hey, Ike, you want to be my partn......................

Epilogue

Calmly comes the peace
Quieted is restless wanderlust
And guilt and loneliness.
The accompanying pain
Gives way to the welcoming glow.
And now, this quietness lays to rest
Another of the tortured souls
Who's firefly spirit flickered here and there,
Attempting to be relevant to the
Senseless other world.
The other world outside,
Where time and space
And goals and accomplishments
Tramp upon the inner spark
That flickered now and then.
The spark set free, now
Upon its quest to light
Another pulse of life upon
Its troubled way, until
The quietness falls again
And lays to rest another
Emanation of the vibrant Force.
A white cold mini-slab marks
The spot, with exact precision
Line and row, as if to force
One last curse of conformity
Upon the troubled, searching
Firefly's spirit glow.

Printed in the United States
53126LVS00002B/6